HARD
Compromise

A COMPROMISE ME NOVEL

HARD
Compromise

A COMPROMISE ME NOVEL

SAMANTHE BECK

Entangled Publishing, LLC
2614 South Timberline Road
Suite 109
Fort Collins, CO 80525
Visit our website at www.entangledpublishing.com.

Brazen is an imprint of Entangled Publishing, LLC. For more information on our titles, visit www.brazenbooks.com.

Edited by Heather Howland
Cover design by Heather Howland
Cover photo by Lindee Robinson, featuring Garrett Pentecost and Daria Rottenberk

Manufactured in the United States of America

First Edition November 2016

ENTANGLED
BRAZEN

To Hud. You're my *Babycakes!*

Prologue

"Slide your sexy self over here, girl. I've got something for you."

The invitation carried despite the thumping beat blasting from the nearby private cabana. Laurie turned her back on the two guys dancing with her on the low, teak table they'd commandeered from the cabana to find the cute blond she'd talked to earlier in the evening staring up at her from the sand. A fresh bottle of champagne dangled from his hand.

The cure for virginity, I hope, because I'm not ending this year without getting laid.

The MBA student from Duke seemed like a qualified candidate for the job. Trent? Brent? One of those. Free-flowing drinks left the details blurry, plus she'd talked to a fraternity's worth of guys tonight. All she knew for sure was they had adorable Southern accents and this one looked like a compact version of the cutie from *The Fast and Furious*.

And he was very smooth. He circulated, turning lots of heads and talking to lots of girls, but every time her glass neared empty, he appeared with a bottle and a charming smile on his face. Flashing her own back at him, she did a little spin and moved closer. The silvery glow of the full moon and illumination from Las Ventanas Resort perched on the bluffs above them cast enough light to let her see his gaze lock on her swaying hips.

The attention felt as good as the music, and her buzz. Yes, she could turn a head, even at a party full of rich, east-coast sorority girls with Ivy-league pedigrees. Getting noticed was pretty much her mission tonight, and she'd dressed accordingly. Her best friend, Chelsea, had sworn the super-short, strategically frayed cut-offs made her ass look legal. Dropping it low, staying on beat—not easy after God knew how much champagne—she held out her glass for a refill. "Thank you."

"My pleasure, sweetheart." He stepped closer and did the honors, while his eyes wandered over her tank top. His focus lingered on her cleavage.

Obviously he was a player, which suited her perfectly because she wanted to play. She was *ready* to play, dammit, but even so, she suddenly wished Chelsea had come with her tonight. Her best friend's levelheaded personality balanced out Laurie's wilder, more restless nature. Chelsea wouldn't stand by and let her make a big mistake. Unfortunately, Chelsea's mom didn't approve of unsupervised beach parties thrown by vacationing frat brothers, and she kept close tabs on her only child. Laurie's mother? Not so much. Denise was too busy running around, drinking, and partying like a porn star to give a crap what her sixteen-year-old daughter was doing. And tonight, her daughter planned to do…everything.

"Are you from around here?" Duke asked.

"Sort of. I'm in my final year at Montenido University." She pointed to the pink university logo stretched across the front of the gray tank top calculated to show off the attention-grabbing curves nature had bestowed last summer. Practically overnight she'd evolved from a girl to a woman. The change sometimes left her feeling like an imposter in her own body.

Tonight she really was an imposter.

Duke's gaze shifted to her face. His brows drew together a little, and a cloud of anxiety formed on the horizon of her mind. "You don't say?"

Her heart sank. Did something about her looks or actions tip him off she didn't belong at this party? Was he going to send her home before the clock struck midnight, like an underaged Cinderella?

"Want to see my student ID? My friend has my wallet, but I'm sure I could find her…" Heat flared in her cheeks at the thought of him calling her bluff. God, she hoped he didn't. She smoothed a hand over her tank top. Tonight's wardrobe played a key role in helping her project a cool, casual twenty-one—or really any age more legit than boring, pointless sixteen. But she'd relied on Chelsea's advice and her own instincts. What if she looked more like a big slutty dork than a college student?

Duke shook his head. "No way, sweetheart. I don't want you going anywhere."

Her pulse settled a bit. "Then I guess I'll stick around."

"Awesome." His smile widened. "So…what's your major?"

Okay, points to Chelsea for suggesting the tank top. She took a gulp of champagne to hide her relief, and a wave of triumph rushed through her, even more dizzying than alcohol. She could answer any way she chose, be anyone she chose. Rebellious Laurie Peterson with her fucked-up mother and penchant for trouble didn't exist here. "I'm a dance major."

To sell the fib, she treated him to some of her better Pussycat Doll moves.

"Damn, girl. I bet you're at the top of your class. I could watch you work that body all night."

All night? Was that some kind of suggestion, or… invitation? Uncertainty anchored her for a moment, but another swallow of champagne sent a fizz of bubbles to her brain and evaporated the caution trying to drag her down. "You could"—she broke off and sipped again—"come up here and dance with me."

He licked his lips. "What'll you give me if I do?"

"What do you want?" She added a slow smile to the end of the question, and even as her palms went sweaty, she prayed she came off grown-up, self-assured—everything she aspired to be.

He handed the bottle of champagne to one of his friends and hopped onto the table. The two guys at the other end of the table jumped down. "How about a kiss?"

"A kiss?" Her heart tripped in her chest, and her attention automatically zoomed in on his mouth. The corners curved upward.

Shit, Laurie, stop staring at his lips like a complete rookie. Act like you've done this millions of times.

The thing was, she hadn't. She'd kissed a few guys, but just high school boys—nobody who actually knew what he was doing. Now was her chance to change that, assuming she didn't screw it up. She downed the last of her drink, tossed the cup to the sand, and turned so she faced him. Finally, she lifted one eyebrow and shot him the cocky look she'd perfected for exactly such an occasion. "Just a kiss?"

"For starters." He stepped closer. "A kiss to kick off the New Year."

Anticipation prickled beneath her skin, but no overwhelming urges of the sort her older, more experienced friends had described. Maybe because, physically at least, he didn't overwhelm her. Despite her bare feet, she and Duke stood almost eye to eye. Then his arms wound around her waist, his hands slipped into the back pockets of her cut-offs, and her cocky faltered. Was it her move now? Should she do the same to him?

His lips found the curve of her neck and his mouth went to work there. Okay, time to do *something*. Only a freaking amateur would just stand there like a statue. She dipped her fingers into the back pockets of his shorts, but…shoot…they were buttoned. Without stopping to think, she yanked the flaps to tug them open. His startled grunt stilled her hands. Crap. She'd accidentally given him a wedgie. Talk about a freaking amateur.

"Sorry!" She jerked her hands away and left them hovering awkwardly at his waist.

"No worries, sweet thing." He pulled her in closer. His chuckle tickled across her collarbone. "I like a woman who's not afraid to go after what she wants."

The teasing words bolstered her confidence. They described exactly the person she longed to be. Not just a *woman*, a fearless woman. She wanted to hold onto this feeling. The crowd around them erupted into a countdown. Heart pounding, she settled her hands on his shoulders and tipped her face up. His features swam into focus and she lowered her eyelids. Seduction 101. "I like a man who does the same," she managed, and parted her lips in silent invitation.

Music swelled. People whooped. Corks popped like a fireworks finale, and champagne rained down on them in sparkling droplets. Duke slowly lowered his head. She inhaled, and waited with baited breath. The moment felt magical. *She* felt magical. Beautiful. Ready for anything. *Definitely the best New Year's Eve ev—*

"Party's over, people. Somebody turn off that music."

The booming voice cut through the noisy celebration. A millisecond later, the music stopped, and a closer voice, equally authoritative, said, "You." A flashlight beam landed on Duke. "Get your hands out of her pants and step down from the table. You"—the beam swung to her—"stay put."

Duke froze. "What the…?"

Big fists came out of nowhere and half-assisted, half-dragged him off the table, leaving her standing, alone, on her pedestal of shame. She rubbed her shoulders to combat a chill, and blinked at the laser show of flashlight beams crisscrossing the night, wielded by a small team of uniformed officers. A short distance away old Sheriff Halloran stood overseeing the activity.

Happy New Year, you're busted.

"Back off, asshole," Duke said, and tried to throw an elbow into the imposing figure still holding his arm.

"*Deputy* Asshole," the voice corrected, not releasing him. "And I want to see some ID."

"Jesus. All right. Sorry." He dug for his wallet, one-handed, and produced what looked like a driver's license. "But seriously, let go, man. I haven't done anything."

The deputy examined the ID under the flashlight. He was bigger than Duke—taller, broader—with a cool assurance Laurie couldn't help but envy. "Are you aware your dance partner's barely old enough to drive?"

"Fuck me." Duke's head swung her way as her shame ripened into mortification.

Sheriff Halloran approached, calm if not a little weary. "Hello, Lauralie. Out past curfew, aren't you?"

Duke turned his attention to Halloran, and started talking fast. "She told me she was in college. How would I know different? Come on, look at her! Shit." His voice took on a desperate edge. "Nothing happened. We danced. That's all." He flung an arm in her direction. "Tell him!"

"Just a dance." She wasn't about to bring up the champagne, or anything else that might lead to Halloran or his cohort placing a call to her mother. Then she'd really be screwed.

"I don't suppose he gave you anything to drink?" Halloran asked.

"No." The denial came fast, and firm, but a loud hiccup followed like an embarrassing parent. A drunk one.

Somebody sighed.

Duke muttered, "Aw, hell," and then took up the cause of rescuing his own ass. "This isn't even my party. I'm just a guest. My room is right up there." He nodded toward the resort. "I didn't rent the cabana, or order the alcohol. None of it. If you want to double check with the resort, they can verify—"

"Tell you what," Halloran interrupted. "You and I are going to take a walk up to the resort and discuss the situation. Deputy, will you deal with Miss Peterson?"

"No problem, assuming she can obey my instructions better than she can obey a curfew."

Cop humor. LOL.

Halloran took her dance partner by the arm and steered him toward the path leading up to the resort. Staring after them made her dizzy, so she lowered her chin to her chest and focused on her bare feet. How embarrassing for Duke, getting perp-walked through a ritzy hotel lobby on New Year's Eve.

But his embarrassment paled compared to the world of hurt she'd be in if Deputy Do-Right decided to Breathalyze her. Her stomach took a sickening spin as she thought about the consequences. Minor in possession of alcohol. Public intoxication. She didn't come from a rich Montenido family who would hire a high-powered attorney to get their teenager out of trouble. Uh-uh. The juvie judge would make an example of her. Definitely yank her driver's permit. She could probably kiss good-bye any chance of getting her actual driver's license until she was at least twenty-one. Oh, God...

Don't panic. Hold your shit together, and act sober.

"Where are your shoes?"

The deputy's question cut short her self-coaching session. She looked up too fast and lost her balance. Gravity dumped her on her ass in the sand, and the impact jostled another incriminating hiccup out of her.

Black shoes appeared in her line of vision a second before she heard the soft pop of a knee joint. He crouched, balanced his weight on his heels, and reached for her arm. "Are you all right, Lauralie?"

She scooted away, which only succeeded in shoveling a load of Nido Beach into her shorts. "Don't call me that." An obscenely loud hiccup tagged along with the retort. So much for holding her shit together. She should have kept her mouth shut, but she couldn't help herself. Only her mother called her Lauralie, and only when she wanted something. And basically, if Denise's mouth was moving, she wanted something.

The flashlight beam landed on her. She flinched under the glare. "Can you get that out of my face?"

He didn't immediately respond, just continued assessing her. A not-particularly-clever wisecrack leaped to her lips, about how a picture would last longer, but the smart-mouthed comment died away as an uncomfortable awareness settled over her. He was looking past the blond hair she'd tamed into smooth waves and her intentionally sophisticated makeup. Past her cocked chin and folded arms. He was looking at *her*. And if he kept looking, he'd see all the things she worked really hard to make sure nobody saw. Insecurities. Fears. Just when she couldn't stand the spotlight of his attention a second longer, he moved the beam off her.

"Those yours, Jailbait?"

More cop humor. Her pink Uggs sat in the small pool of light. "Yes."

He stood, and helped her to her feet before she could scramble up under her own power. Sand showered from her shorts, subsiding to a drizzle as he marched her over to her shoes. The last thing she needed was more in there, so rather than sit, she bent forward and reached for her boot. Bad choice, because tonight's festivities left her less than steady. She started to topple.

A strong hand closed on her arm, just above her elbow, and righted her as if she weighed nothing. "Get them on. I've got you."

The heat from his palm made her realize how cold she was. Numb and clumsy and freezing cold. She tugged her boots on, moving as fast as she could because shivers threatened.

"Anything else you need to collect before we go, Lauralie?"

"No, and I told you not to call me that." Even in her current state, she winced at the bitchy tone in her voice.

"It's your name, right?" he responded, seemingly unperturbed. He kept his hold on her as they walked down the beach to the parking lot.

"You sure know a lot about me. My name. My age."

"Halloran tipped me off before he sent me over to reel you in."

"And *you* are?"

"Ethan Booker."

"Ethan Booker of the Montenido Bookers?" But she didn't need him to confirm her guess. Now that she had the frame of reference it wasn't hard to superimpose this badge-wearing badass over her pre-teen memory of an athletic high-school hottie striding out of the surf with a board under his arm and a bunch of girls waiting by his towel. Golden-boy came from a wealthy, high-profile family. And wealthy by Montenido standards meant mega-fucking-rich.

"Ethan Booker of the Montenido Sheriff's Department,"

he shot back. There was just enough sharpness in the reply to tell her she might have struck a nerve—like maybe he didn't like money and privilege being the first thing people associated with him.

Defensive instincts had her pressing on the point, to see just how sore it was. "Please. Your family's loaded. Why slum it in the sheriff's department?"

"How else would I get to meet underaged girls who are about to be grounded until they're thirty?"

Grounded? What kind of *Gilmore Girls* world did he think she lived in? She cleared her tight throat. "Are you going to a-arrest me?"

"We're going to consider tonight a warning. Don't tempt me to change my mind."

Relief reduced her to silence. She couldn't even manage a thank you, for fear he'd hear a telltale quiver in her voice. He led her around to the passenger side of the cruiser, opened the door, and stood there while she got in. "Seat belt," he prompted, and then shut the door. Something about the way he handled her made her feel taken care of. Not a normal feeling for her, and more than a little unsettling. She straightened, crossed her arms, and pulled on her I-can-take-care-of-myself cloak.

He got behind the wheel, and flicked the interior light to the brightest setting. Then he turned to her. "Buckle—Fuck, I'm going to kill that prick."

His eyes were glued to her throat. She flipped the visor down to see her reflection in the vanity mirror, and sucked in a shocked breath. The sexy Jessica Simpson-style waves she'd tried to emulate hung around her face in tangles. The shadow, liner, and mascara she'd painstakingly applied earlier tonight ringed her eyes like dirty smudges. And the cherry on the cake of all this classy? A big, red bruise blooming on the side of her neck. A souvenir from Duke. She couldn't even feel the stupid thing, but it looked pathetic. *She* looked pathetic. Used. Cheap.

Her euphoria from just before midnight came back to mock her. There was nothing magical or beautiful about the girl staring back at her in the mirror. A sour taste percolated in the back of her throat as another thought struck.

She looked *exactly* like her mother.

The impulse to hide had her hunching her shoulders and twisting toward the window, but Booker caught her chin. "Lauralie, look at me."

A cold, hard ball of humiliation lodged in her throat. Her chest tightened. She pulled her gaze up, and fell into dark, concerned eyes.

"Did he hurt you?"

The tattered edges of her imaginary cloak of self-sufficiency slipped out of her grasp. She burst into tears.

He immediately released her, and scrubbed his hand over his face. "Shit. All right. Everybody relax. I'm not touching you. Nobody's going to touch you. I'm just going to ask you some questions, and I want you to answer honestly. Are you okay?"

Okay? Try fucked up, embarrassed, and angry—mostly with herself. Her teeth chattered, and she couldn't stop shaking, but as far as how he meant? Basically yes. "I-I'm f-f-fine."

"Then why are you crying?"

The careful tone of his question made her cry harder. People weren't careful with her. She wasn't even careful with herself, and the reasons were hard to explain in a way that made sense—especially to someone like Booker, who'd never longed to change who he was or where he came from. She racked her brain for a reply that wouldn't sound so crazy. A night like tonight gave a girl plenty of reasons to cry, but she settled for one of her more immediate worries. "If Denise finds out about tonight, she's not going to ground me. She's going to kick my ass out. All she wants is a reason to justify booting me. "

"Denise Peterson is your mother?"

Clearly, Denise's reputation preceded her. What a shock. "Uh-huh." A tissue would be handy right now, but the neckline of her tank top worked. She wiped her eyes, cringing at the mess left behind on the light-gray cotton. "Neither of us is particularly proud of the fact, but yeah, she is."

"Is she going to be home when we get there?"

"Doubtful." She sniffed to battle the tears trying to escape through her sinuses, but then gave up and wiped her nose, too. What the hell? At this point he wasn't likely to mistake her for Miss America.

He stared out the windshield, but something in the set of his jaw told her he was considering the options. She held her breath as the silence stretched. He hadn't challenged her obvious lie about not drinking. Hadn't subjected her to a sobriety test, or arrested her, but it was probably too much to hope he'd let the whole incident slide without informing her parent.

"You're sixteen, dammit. That guy was twenty-five." Frustration reverberated in his voice. "Do you even realize how wrong that is? If you can't keep yourself in check, someone needs to do it for you."

"Denise isn't that someone," she whispered. "Please. I won't do it again. I promise."

Serious eyes drilled into hers. Then he shook his head, and let out a low, resigned sigh. "Jailbait, this is your one and only free pass. I told you we'd consider tonight a warning, so listen up, because here it comes. I'm going to be watching you from now on. If you stray over the line in any way, shape, or form I'm going to bust your little ass so hard your head will spin. Understand?"

As if she'd say no. He had her boxed in, and they both knew it. Even so, some of the pressure in her chest loosened. Boxed in by Booker felt oddly secure. More like a safety measure than a shackle. She nodded.

"Good. What's your address?"

She gave it to him, and then wrapped her arms around her middle for warmth and sat in the darkness as he drove to Nido Terrace—the ghetto of Montenido. An occasional shiver still rattled her teeth. After a mile he muttered a curse, aimed the vents her way, and punched up the heat. Otherwise, they traveled in silence.

Every so often she snuck a peek at him. He'd graduated from high school the same year as her friend Heidi, which made him a few years younger than the guy from the beach. But while Duke still had the lean, narrow build of a college boy, Booker was all grown up. She stole a glance at his lap from beneath lowered lashes, and swallowed. Definitely grown up.

Her gaze fled the imposing bulge and landed on his profile, taking in the slope of his forehead, the masculine angle of his nose, and his square chin. His cheekbone created a sexy parallel line with his jaw. He was cuter than Duke. No. Wrong word. Cute implied boyish, and nobody looking at Booker saw a boy. They saw a man. A girl in search of a guy who knew what he was doing could do worse. A lot worse.

He must have sensed her staring, because he glanced at her. She turned away, caught her reflection in the side mirror, and realized she was chewing the ragged cuticle around her thumb—a nervous habit she'd picked up from Denise. Forcing herself to stop, she put her hands to better use finger-combing some life into her hair, and then scrubbing away the traces of makeup under her eyes. Those little efforts helped. She looked more like her normal self. Then again, was that really helpful?

No. Not when it comes to a guy like Booker.

The depressing thought backhanded her, and left a lingering ache of truth. What did she really have going for her, other than the ability to fill out a tank top and cut-offs? Booker's hard-to-read expression didn't offer any indication he'd noticed those particular talents. Did he see anything in her except a troublemaker?

Why do you care?

She couldn't explain why, but she did. She wanted him to like her. The car rolled to the curb in front of her house. He killed the engine and the lights. "This it?"

"Uh-huh." Her pulse quickened. Could she *make* him like her?

While she worked on a strategy, he came around and opened her door. She climbed out and turned to him. Moonlight and shadows played over his face.

Go after what you want, her internal voice insisted. *Work with what you've got.* She straightened to full height, which still only brought her even with his chin, and eased her shoulders back to put the girls front and center. Then she inhaled deeply, hoping his gaze might slide down. It didn't.

"How can I thank you for being so decent tonight?"

Her voice sounded a little hesitant, but it could pass for breathlessness rather than nerves.

"By staying out of trouble." No hesitation there.

She took a step closer, so her breasts almost touched his chest. "I meant some way I could thank you right here and now."

He retreated a half step, which offered zero encouragement. But now that she'd put herself out there, she couldn't seem to find a graceful way to back down. She stared up at him, and slowly ran the tip of her tongue over her upper lip. "Think about it."

"I'm thinking about a lot of things, Jailbait, such as how,

unlike your friend from the beach, I know the difference between a girl and a woman. Go home."

Rejection stung. It stung a lot when it came from a mom who treated her like a stray dog, but it stung coming from Booker, too. "That's it? Just, 'Go home?'"

He nodded, and then added insult to injury by pinching her chin, and giving her the barest trace of a smile. "Do us all a favor and pick on someone your own size for a while."

Embarrassment, and—if she was honest with herself—relief, filtered through her. But she wasn't in the mood to be honest, or to be treated like a child. She had to stop herself from stamping her foot. "For how long?"

Firm hands closed on her shoulders and turned her around. He gave her a little push toward the house.

"We can revisit the topic in ten years."

Chapter One

"Bugger me, Booker. You've been lusting after one woman for ten years?" Booker's soon-to-be brother-in-law's voice held a note of incredulity even the windy ride in the convertible Jag couldn't cover.

"I've *known* her for ten years," Booker corrected, and stared at the full moon shining down on him like an interrogator's spotlight from the unrelenting blackness of night sky. "Lust didn't factor in for the first few. When I was a rookie, she was Montenido's poster girl for at-risk teens—a high-school kid with the body of a bikini model, zero parental supervision, and a rebellious streak a mile wide. I felt protective, because she attracted every predatory asshole within a fifty-mile radius, and she was too young to know better."

"Okay," Aaron inclined his shaved head, and moonlight glanced off the ladder of silver rings studding his right ear, "I stand corrected. But after she graduated?"

Yes, after that his protective instincts had turned into something trickier, because he'd been forced to face the maddening reality he could no longer bust any adult male who came sniffing around. But for him, she'd still been off-limits. "You mean when she was eighteen and I was twenty-four?"

Aaron had the decency to wince, because despite the shaved head, beard, tats, and tendency to swear like a sailor—albeit a British one—his moral compass aimed due North. "Point taken. Still, somewhere between past and present, you never thought, 'Now's the bloody time'?"

Sure he had. Sometime during the last handful of years, Booker's life had become an exercise in self-restraint as he'd watched her sample men like candy. Fair enough. She deserved a chance to indulge her curiosity. Life had afforded him the same opportunity, and he'd taken full advantage.

She'd never shown an interest in going back for seconds, which made it easier to bide his time, but the I-dare-you flicker in her eyes every time she glanced his way told him he wasn't the only one feeling the pull between them. Pull or no, he wasn't interested in being the flavor of the night, so timing counted.

"Now's the time," he muttered.

"Huh?" Aaron pulled up to a four-way stop behind a red Mercedes. "What are you going to do, wankstain? Make the turn or sit there and blink your signal all night?"

Booker ignored the rhetorical questions aimed at the driver in front of them. The past twelve months, he'd found himself running out of noble reasons to resist the temptation of Lauralie Peterson. Now, he was flat out. He couldn't tell himself she was still playing. She'd gotten serious—professionally, at least. She'd opened Babycakes Bakery, and invested every bit of her talent, energy, and hard-earned capital into it. With her business taking off, he figured she was ready to bring a similar sense of purpose to her personal life.

Well, *ready* might be an overstatement. The woman had

an inborn pride that demanded she always stand on her own two feet. She wasn't an island, mind you. She had friends. She had family—the fucked-up variety, but still, the ties existed. Yet heaven forbid she need anyone.

She had to get past that particular hang-up, because there was going to be need between them. A whole hell of a lot of need. He'd do his damnedest to satisfy every one of hers, but when he'd resolved to make this the year he tugged on the invisible tether binding them, he'd known getting close would bring a crash course in need. For both of them.

Odds seemed good she'd require a push. Fine. He knew how to push, and he knew when.

"Now's the time," he repeated, a little louder. When he'd hauled her underaged ass home from Nido Beach on New Year's Eve a decade ago, and refused her reckless offer to show her appreciation, he'd told her they could revisit the topic in ten years. At the time, he'd tossed the answer out as a way to brush her back, and emphasize how much growing up she still had to do regardless of how physically mature she looked. But ten years had turned into…well…ten fucking years, and time was up. Tonight.

"Far be it for me to criticize a man's timing, but did you not just spend the better part of the evening going shot-for-shot with my bride-to-be?"

Booker glanced over in time to catch the look Aaron cast at him. "So?"

"So, no offense, mate, but you may not be in the best shape to make your move."

"What, you think I'm impaired?"

"I reckon, yeah, and it would serve you right. What kind of plonker gets shitfaced with his sister on New Year's Eve?"

"I didn't get shitfaced. And for the record, *she* challenged *me*. If she hadn't been cheerleading Mom's efforts to pair me up with an eligible bachelorette of her choosing in time for the wedding, I wouldn't have resorted to drinking her under the table." When Kate had tossed out the bet—if she downed the most shots, she got to pick his date for the wedding—he'd willingly cracked the seal on the bottle himself. His sister was notoriously overconfident when it came to wagers. A hundred and twenty pounds and a preference for wine ensured him an easy victory, and the only thing four shots of Jack prevented him from doing tonight was getting behind the wheel. "I only wish my mother was as easily outmaneuvered."

"Your mum didn't build Best Life into a billion dollar brand by being easily outmaneuvered," Aaron noted.

"No, she did not. She got there by being bossy as hell and thinking she knows what's best for everyone. And now, thanks to you and Kate infecting her with wedding fever, she's decided what's best for me is a trip down the aisle. It's past time she accepted a simple fact—I don't need her help managing my life." He folded his arms. "I've got my own plans."

"About your so-called plans…are you storming into this party with your balls out and your guns blazing, or shall we aim for something a tad more discreet?"

"You get rid of the guests. I'll handle the rest." He could already picture her, breathless and ready as he braced her against the nearest surface and unleashed half a decade's worth of repressed longings. Fuck her so thoroughly she'd have no standing to dismiss the event as a heat-of-the-moment hookup. He was coming for her. *Her*, dammit, and he hadn't waited this long only to be shown the door after one energetic encounter.

So yes, he'd use the chemistry to land him in her bed, but from there it was on him to convince her the connection between them couldn't simply be sweated out of their systems. He had to get it through her hard head and fortified heart that he intended to stick around, and figure out where "they" led.

Storming in tonight with the element of surprise on his side might work. Or it might blow up in his face. Either way, he was done waiting.

Aaron's eyes widened as he pulled to the curb in front of her apartment. People milled on the front lawn, and the small porch. Music blasted from the open windows of her ground-floor unit, layering over the sounds of laughter and conversation. "Oh, sure. I'll just wave my magic wand and make everyone disappear."

"Delaney's is within walking distance. Drinks are on you. Say it loud and then step aside."

"You want me to buy drinks for fifty friggin' people?"

He didn't flinch. "You want to marry my sister?"

"I'll dance to this tune until Valentine's Day, Book, but once she says 'I do' the 'want-to-marry-my-sister?' shite ends, and I'm no longer your wench."

Booker smiled and popped the door. "I count six long weeks between now and February fourteenth. Lead the way, wench."

He had a woman to claim.

. . .

"Sounds like you've got the whole town packed into your apartment."

Laurie pushed the phone to her ear to hear over the din of the party. She wasn't about to let a little logistical challenge like Chelsea's recent move to Maui for work keep them from ringing in the New Year together. "It's a little bigger than I planned." Behind her, a cork exploded out of a bottle, followed by an approving roar of appreciation. "And louder. But what the hell, it's New Year's Eve, and…hey—!"

She broke off as a helpful soul refilled her flute, and splashed a liberal amount of ice-cold Korbel down the front of her silver sequin top in the process. The white, silk shorts that ended high on her thighs fared better, thank God, because one errant spill and those suckers would be see-through. Her strappy, silver heels survived unscathed—though the same couldn't be said for her protesting arches. As soon as the party ended, she planned to ditch the sandals.

Normally she might invite someone to help her work the kinks out. A strapping candidate with strong hands, who knew when to be gentle, when to be firm, and when to advance a foot rub to a full-body massage, but more and more lately only one man sprang to mind, and he was absolutely out of the question, as well as not in attendance, so… Her doorbell chimed, ringing through the chaos of music and laughter.

"Shit." She plucked her top away from her chest and started toward her door even as the nearest guest pulled it open.

"Everything okay?" Chelsea asked.

"Nothing a trip to the dry cleaner won't fix… *Shit*."

"What now?"

Had she conjured him with one unguarded thought? Maybe, because a breath-stealing span of shoulders filled her doorframe. "I don't believe this. Booker's darkening my doorstep."

"Ethan Booker? *Sheriff* Ethan Booker?"

"Yes, and yes." Not in uniform, no, but otherwise looking as authoritative, and—damn her perverse hormones—*hot* as ever in a charcoal V-neck that did all kinds of justice to his shoulders and chest, and dark pants that did justice to everything else. The porch light found the sun-streaked strands in his thick brown hair and turned them copper.

"What do you think he wants?"

"No clue."

Perverse or not, no red-blooded woman could deny Booker was an eyeful, but she ought to be used to it. She'd been looking her fill for a while. In the years since rookie Booker had first hauled her sorry ass home from Nido Beach, he'd worked his way up the ladder of command to sheriff, and she'd outgrown her juvenile rebellions. Mostly. She owned a business, paid taxes, and, aside from a few speeding tickets, abided by the laws like any upstanding member of society. Didn't matter. Booker's assessing stare always regressed her to teenaged troublemaker at the same time it sent her grown-up sex-drive surging.

She was no longer a wayward delinquent resorting to reckless behavior in a desperate search for the attention she didn't get at home, but only a blind woman would miss the fact that he saw a shadow of that girl when he looked at her. And he looked at her a lot. As if he knew exactly what his quiet stare did to her. As if he was biding his time.

"Think he got a noise complaint?" Chelsea asked.

All her neighbors were here, so it seemed unlikely, but she raised her chin and channeled the defiance she defaulted to whenever Booker appeared. "So what if he did? It's New Year's Eve, for God's sake."

While she watched, those keen eyes scanned the room. For her.

Someone killed the music, and people started cheering.

Ten… The walls of her apartment shook as revelers broke into the countdown. "Ten lousy seconds and the party will be over anyway. What's the point of barging in now, except to be a hard-ass?"

Nine… "Maybe he wants to wish you a happy New Year?"

Eight… "Yeah, right. From a jail cell."

Seven… Booker's attention locked on her. Her stomach took a free fall, as usual. She realized she was worrying the corner of her thumbnail and made herself cut it out.

Six… "Uh-oh. He spotted me." His gaze turned oddly… purposeful. No other word fit the lowered brows and tractor-beam stare. The man was clearly on a mission, and the determination in his expression raised the tiny hairs on her arm. Whatever he wanted, it had nothing to do with a noise complaint. Booker's voice echoed through her mind from a full decade ago. *We can revisit the topic in ten years.*

Five… "Don't assume the worst."

Four… She downed her champagne, and set the glass on an end table while he shouldered his way through her small, packed living room. Her rapid pulse rushed the bubbles straight to her head.

Three… "I better go."

Two… "Happy New Year. Call me tomorrow, okay?"

One… "I may only get one phone call. Happy New Year's, Chels."

Booker took her phone, hit disconnect, and slipped it into his back pocket at the same time confetti went flying and the room erupted into shouts of "Happy New Year!"

"Hey, give me my pho—"

His mouth crashed down on hers. Strong fingers sank into her hair, and…holy hell. However many years she'd had to envision this moment, one thing became startlingly apparent. She'd failed to adequately prepare for it. Waves of excitement and alarm rolled through her at the realization.

Then again, how could she have prepared for Booker's kiss? How could she prepare for this much intensity, and all this *hunger*?

His mouth moved on hers, parting her lips wider, then wider still, and just when she'd gotten a grip on his shoulders and started to make a move of her own, he swept in with long, deep strokes she couldn't resist. Didn't want to resist. And he was so sure she wouldn't he didn't even hurry, simply kept up the slow, commanding slide of his tongue. She didn't consider herself the kind of woman who obeyed commands, but he was dragging them somewhere she desperately wanted to go.

A place she'd fantasized about for too long. Though it wasn't smart, or particularly sane, she took two fistfuls of his very nice, very expensive sweater, and held on.

From somewhere nearby, a voice yelled, "Take it to the pub, yanks. First round's on me." In a vague recess of her mind, she registered people leaving, calling their thanks as they squeezed past, but she didn't respond. More urgent priorities demanded her attention. Priorities like the scrape of his rough jaw against her skin, and whisper-soft cashmere covering hard muscles. Her hands found a route under his sweater and raced along his warm, smooth, withstand-anything back.

"Aaand we're out. Cheers to you. Happy New Year." The door closed, and she sensed without looking they had the apartment to themselves. Apparently he sensed it too, because the next thing she knew, he'd backed her up against the hallway wall. He pulled his mouth away long enough to level a serious look at her. "Ground rules."

"Uh-uh." Rules would require negotiation, and negotiation implied they had more at stake here than rampant lust. In other words, negotiation would ruin this. She wrapped her arms around his neck, came up on her toes, and sank her teeth into his upper lip. He groaned, and slammed his hips into hers. The position pinned her to the wall, and gave her a forceful preview of what he had in store for her. Her body responded with a rush of anticipation guaranteed to send her silk shorts to the dry cleaners along with her champagne-splashed top. Against the lip she'd just abused, she murmured, "Booker, don't confuse me with one of your well-bred, easily-shocked, country-club girls. I'm not well-bred and nothing shocks me. My only rules are fast, hard, and so filthy dirty it leaves a stain on your soul."

Chapter Two

Her words put to rest ground rule number one. Express mutual consent. Too bad the accord he sought involved a hell of a lot more than fast, hard, and dirty. He pushed her wild mane of blond corkscrew curls back from her forehead, framed her face with his hands—okay, trapped her—and waited until she looked him in the eye. Hers brimmed with impatience, which made him all the more determined to go slow. "Declining a review of the ground rules constitutes your agreement to everything I've got in mind."

The smart-ass gave him a wide-eyed, innocent look. "My goodness, Sheriff. Are you going to whip out your cuffs and restrain me? Push me up against the wall and give me a thorough frisking?" Her smile returned, sly and defiant. "Should I assume the position while you unholster your big, dangerous weapon?"

Graphic images played in his mind, and challenged his commitment to go slow. Some things hadn't changed in ten years. She still liked to test the boundaries. He held his ground and returned her cagey smile. "You've given this a lot of thought, haven't you, Lauralie?"

Her eyes narrowed, and her little nose went up a notch. "Don't call me that—"

"Shhh." He pressed a firm kiss against her stubborn mouth. "No rules, remember?"

He used his tongue to sweep the next smart-assed comment out of her mouth. The methodology worked, but took a toll on him, too. He'd dreamed about having her pressed against him like this, and those dreams always proved he had a vivid, masochistic imagination, but nothing his subconscious mind had manufactured came anywhere close to reality.

"You smell like vanilla." The sweet scent clung to skin that was warmer, silkier, and more sensitive than in his darkest fantasies. Her lips were far more giving, and nothing, absolutely nothing, compared to her taste. He promised himself he'd savor every inch of her before the sun rose.

"Occupational hazard."

"I like it."

Slim fingers skidded down the front of his trousers. She moaned approvingly—thank Christ, because his cock had reached zipper-straining proportions and there was no camouflaging it—"I see that you do. What else do you like?"

Before he could answer, she reached lower and cupped his balls. Not a polite, gentle cradling, but a hold tight enough to wring a groan out of him. Then she squeezed, and while a paralyzing mix of pain and pleasure shot through his groin, she managed to undo his belt and unfasten his pants.

Blinking the haze from of his vision, he clamped his fingers around her wrist. "I've waited a long time. Don't even think about rushing." He caught her other wrist, and pinned her arms to the wall over her head.

Her pent-up breath gushed out against his cheek. He breathed it in, absorbing her through every available means, then banded her wrists in one hand and brought the other down in a long, sweeping caress from the bend in her elbow to the swell of her breast. He loitered there, memorizing the tantalizing curve beneath the spangled top. No bra. The discovery sent currents of need scorching through him, followed by an annoying afterburn of jealousy. Irrational jealousy, he silently acknowledged, as he lifted her breast and let it fall. A million shiny, silver disks shimmered. She bit her lip, and arched off the wall for more of his touch—*his* touch—but the possessive emotion refused to back off.

"Did you plan to torment every guy at the party with the sight of your tits bouncing around under your shirt, or were you aiming to torment one in particular?" He punctuated the question with a quick slap to the side of the lush swell. She rewarded him with a breathy moan, and an involuntary twist of her hips.

"Like everything else I do, I dress to please *me*." She tipped her head, and aimed defiant eyes at him.

Defiant or not, the truth in the words restored his equilibrium—marginally—even as they riled his curiosity. "Going bareback pleases you?"

"Sometimes," she replied, drawing the word out in her huskiest voice and lowering her long lashes.

A calculated maneuver, but still 100 percent effective. And her smile told him she damn well knew it.

"My tits are very sensitive. Each sequin in this top is anchored by a little knot, and when they shift, I feel it against my skin. It's incredibly...stimulating."

The visual stimulated *him* to no end. The slim cords in her arms tensed, testing his hold on her wrists. Not frantically. More like an obligatory escape attempt. He thwarted her, catching how the small show of force sped her pulse. This stimulated her, too, at least to a point. Fiercely independent Lauralie got an illicit thrill from feeling a little dominated. How far could he take that? He rubbed his chest over the fancy shirt, just enough to disturb the sequins.

An uncensored, completely uncalculated noise came from the back of her throat. Honest and needy. Too honest for her comfort, apparently, because this time she tried to break his hold for real. He knew exactly the moment she realized she couldn't, and counted down the seconds until…

"No fair."

Quite a sight she made, with her enormous, artfully-smudged eyes flashing, and remnants of some shiny, pink gloss still decorating her swollen lips. "Fairness implies rules. I could have sworn you said 'no rules.'"

"Screw you, Booker."

"Don't worry, we'll get to that, but I've got a score to settle first." He whispered the promise in one unprotected ear, and then kissed his way along her tense jaw. At the same time, he eased his hand under her shirt, up her slender ribs, to take the weight of her breast. "You can dish it out, but…" he squeezed. Not quite as tightly as she'd tormented his balls…"can you take it?"

The way she drilled the tight peak into the center of his hand gave him his answer, even before she said, "Harder."

She wanted harder. He wanted her off balance and begging. He swept the top up her body, releasing his hold on her wrists long enough to drag the thing off, and toss it aside. She stood there—pinned—with her arms stretched high and those sensitive tits she loved to please lifted toward him like a gift.

Just to make her wait…make her want…he took his time appreciating the view while her chest rose and fell with quick, urgent breaths.

"Booker—"

"How hard?"

"What?"

The impatience in her voice made him smile. "How hard

do you like to be handled?"

She cocked her head and gave him an imperious look. "Do I look like the kind of girl you need to be gentle with?"

In answer, he braced his forearms against the wall, leaned in, and slowly, deliberately let his sweater graze her nipples. To his satisfaction, she nearly dissolved. Her eyelids drifted down, her cheeks flushed, and her breath hitched on a helpless sound.

"Was that a whimper?"

"Uh-uh."

"Really? It sounded like a whimper to me. Next time, I'll —"

"No." She shook her head. "No next time."

"Next time," he continued, ignoring her interruption because there sure as hell would be a next time, "I'll spend days teasing your tits like this, just to hear you whimper for me again, but now"—he released her wrists and lifted her until he brought his head level with her straining nipples— "I'm going to taste them."

She gripped his shoulder with one hand, plunged the other into his hair, and arched up, trying to take control. "Finally."

Resisting her attempt to use him to her satisfaction, he rested his mouth against one pink crest. "Patience, Lauralie," he murmured, and gave her the barest of kisses. She let loose a strangled curse. Her nipple throbbed between his lips. Her knees turned into a vice, and the back of her head hit plaster. He kept the kisses slow, and the pull light, until she writhed against the wall with feverish grace.

Gentle worked for her, regardless of what she claimed. Time to see how rough she liked it. He gradually increased the depth and suction of each kiss, filling his mouth, allowing his teeth to score her skin. Her body lifted toward his, as if connected by a network of wires running from her nipple to the farthest reaches of her nervous system. When she panted his name, he kissed his way to the other breast, and lashed his tongue along the underside until she shoved herself into his mouth. He lavished the same attention, sucking gently, then not so gently, then gently again, enjoying how she alternated between showering him with praise and damning him to hell.

Music to his ears. Agony to his dick. He wanted to be inside her more than he wanted his next breath, but he'd endure. If he gave in to the urgency, as soon as he pulled out she'd reduce this to a one-night stand. Easy to compartmentalize and dismiss. He wouldn't allow her do it. He'd push past her barriers, even if need tore at him. Even if they both crawled away a little worse for wear by the time he finished. He intended to share more with her than an orgasm. Or a series of orgasms. Though drawing one out of her now, just to make sure she knew how effectively he could, seemed like a good place to start. Releasing her, he dropped to his knees, and pulled at her slippery white shorts. They caught on the flare of her hips. "How do I — ?"

"Back here," she gasped, already reaching behind her. "There's a zipper — "

That's all the information he needed. He spun her around, gaining ridiculous satisfaction from her startled, "Oh!" It took less than a second to rip the zipper down, and drag the weightless fabric out of his way. The shorts pooled around the ankles of the metallic cock-teasers some designer had the balls to call shoes.

Lace as delicate as a butterfly's wing stretched across the span of her hips, framing the graceful curves along the top of her ass, and delving into the valley between flawless, unprotected cheeks. Hard to believe she hadn't planned that view for someone. Out of line as they were, the territorial thoughts returned in full force.

While he watched, goose bumps rose on her skin. To torture them both, he pressed a kiss to the small of her back, then to the divot on one side of her spine, and then the twin on the other side. She sighed. Fidgeted.

"Who'd you wear these skimpy panties for?"

"Me," she shot back. "They're pretty. I like the way they fit."

"You like having a thin strip of lace wedged all up in here?" He plucked the strip in question and let it snap back into place.

"Yes," she gasped. "Don't you think it looks good?"

She looked fucking amazing, and he had a primitive urge to make sure nobody else enjoyed the sight. Ever. He leaned in and scraped his teeth over bare skin until he snagged the line of lace just above where it disappeared from view. A jerk of his head rent the fabric. He opened his jaw and let the ruined lingerie drop to the floor.

"Oh my God." The wall muffled her voice, but nothing could disguise the way her legs trembled. "Did you just tear my underwear off with your teeth?"

"I owe you a new pair. Now answer my question, or three guesses where my teeth go next." He menaced the plushest part her ass cheek with his incisors.

"Get over yourself, Booker. I wore them for me."

He couldn't get over himself. He wanted to hear her say his name, even if it wasn't true. His frustrated growl gave her fair warning, but all she managed was an edgy cry when he sank his teeth into one ripe, peach-like curve. He snuck his fingers between her thighs, and curled them, barely brushing hot, damp, unbelievably soft flesh before she bucked away.

"Don't," he warned, and gripped a cheek in each hand. "Put your forehead to the wall, close your eyes, say a prayer— whatever you need to do—but don't you dare hold anything back from me. That's one of those ground rules you didn't need to review. Now let's try this again. Who'd you wear the panties for?"

"For me," she insisted, stubborn as ever.

"Wrong answer." He bit the other cheek, and worked two fingers between her legs again. She stiffened, then let out another groan, and opened for him, as far as the shorts around her ankles permitted. He took advantage, stroking, parting, easing his thumb into her tight, hot center and sweeping the inner wall while he rubbed her clit with his knuckle. Firm muscles bunched and released under his lips. Her breath came in ragged bursts.

"Who'd you think of while you slid those panties on and guided them along here?" He flicked his tongue over the path.

She wiggled, but the wall prevented her from getting far. "Nobody—"

His delving tongue dissolved her reply into an inarticulate plea.

Some misplaced sense of propriety, or the intensity of the sensations, forced her onto her toes. He simply tightened the trap, and kept at her—using his tongue, teeth, and fingers to exploit every unprotected part of her. One of her hands slapped the plaster, the other reached back and tangled in his hair.

"It hurts. I have to come so bad it hurts."

The pain definitely cut both ways, but he drew it out a little longer. "Who'd you imagine getting you out of your panties tonight?"

"I didn't…I can't *think*." Her fingers tightened in his hair. Pulling. Demanding. "I need."

Growling his frustration, he scraped his jaw across her satiny ass. "Tell me" He circled his thumb as he pushed in deeper, searching out the hidden place that couldn't withstand direct contact.

Her whole body stiffened when he hit it. She froze there for a suspended heartbeat, and then pounded the wall with her fist as the first spasm shook her. The next unlocked her voice, and words came forth with the same rushing honesty as her orgasm. "You, Booker. *You*. God help me, I thought of you."

Chapter Three

Textured plaster pressed into Laurie's forehead, but all she could do was cling to the wall and gasp lungful after lungful of air while shockwaves raced through her system. What the *hell* had just happened to her?

Ethan Booker just happened to you. He branded your ass, and then handed you the most cataclysmic orgasm of your life. Oh, and then he made you admit you'd envisioned him doing it.

The frightening thing was she hadn't even realized the truth until the words were out, echoing in her ears. How had he known that while she'd dressed for this evening, deep in some forbidden part of her mind, she'd banked on those words he'd spoken ten years ago? She'd secretly fantasized about him being the one to strip off her carefully planned party clothes and show her a Happy New Year.

He's going do it again, if you don't watch yourself.

Good lord, he was. Even now, while she struggled to reclaim control of herself, his big hand lingered between her legs, cupping her in his wide, capable palm. Petting her gently.

Painfully gentle. She'd had no idea such a sensation existed, until now, and she'd had no idea she was so susceptible to it. Worse, his mouth cruised along her hip, and she was pretty sure his lips formed a smile. A smug smile.

That got her moving. She pushed off the wall. He pushed her right back against it, and held her there, hands at her waist, while he took his time running his tongue up her spine, slowly rising to his feet as he worked his way from the small of her back to the nape of her neck. His hand glided down her stomach, and reasserted his claim to the domain between her thighs. She braced for his penetrating touch, but he didn't intrude past her body's damp, swollen barriers. He simply rested there, heavy, proprietary, and strangely…protective. Almost comforting. As if he understood at this moment her orgasm-flushed center needed the refuge.

Protective? Comforting? Holy hell, Peterson, what is wrong with you?

Nothing a little distance wouldn't solve, but just as she reformed her intention to shake him off, he bit her earlobe, sending a warning shiver directly to parts of her still stinging from similar treatment. "Be still. We're not done."

Maybe not, but she turned her head away, trying not to make it too easy for him.

"Unless…" He trailed off and buried his face in her hair. His chest expanded against her shoulder blades as he inhaled, and the shivers threatened again at the notion of him breathing her in like oxygen.

"Unless what?" Pride had her attempting to straighten.

"Unless you can't handle anymore?"

He moved closer. Beneath the chafe of his pants she felt a whole lot "more," and new heat flooded to where he cupped her. Would he detect it? Would he realize he exerted more control over her body with one simple shift of his hips than she did with all the warning lights flashing in her brain? The thought sent a separate wave of heat to her face.

She fell back on old defenses. Sarcasm. Swagger. "Maybe I'm just not particularly interested in what else you've got?"

The insinuation spurred his fingers into action. He administered one long, leisurely stroke and her body betrayed her with wet sounds. His laugh turned her cheeks fiery. "Liar," he scolded.

A pathetic moan slid past her throat, and his hand immediately stilled. "But I can't help wondering if you've hit your limit, because these gorgeous legs of yours are trembling."

Okay, this bit of cockiness she could rectify right now. "My legs are trembling because these shoes are killing my feet."

"Well, now I feel guilty, since you wore them for me."

Shit. She was never going to live that down. Before she could think up a suitably biting reply, he continued, "If you ask nicely, I'll give you some relief."

"This may come as a shock to you, but I know how to take off my shoes all by myself."

"The shoes stay on. I have plans for them. The relief I have in mind involves getting you off your feet. Would you be more comfortable on your knees, or your back? Maybe you prefer a position where you can bury your face in a pillow to keep the entire complex from hearing how *relieved* you are."

His words made her legs tremble all the more, because she had a sneaking suspicion his version of "relief" might feel a lot like torture. Very addictive torture. Time to dole out a little of her own, before she found herself on the receiving end of another crippling orgasm. She pushed her hips back, and rubbed them over the front of his trousers, side to side, and then up, up…sweet Jesus…up, and down. A low growl rumbled up from his chest, and then his hands flew to her waist, fingers digging into her skin. But he didn't stop her.

"Seems like you're in need of some relief, too, Booker. Why don't we move this to the sofa, and I can take care of both our needs?"

With the suddenness of a lightning strike, he spun her around, and fused his mouth to hers. His quick hands got a tight grip on her ass. Strong arms flexed, and the next thing she knew their heads were level, her breasts crushed against cashmere covered granite, and her toes dangled a foot off the ground. Strategies flew out of her head like startled birds, leaving only instincts. She twined her arms around his head. The world spun as he swung away from the wall, and she wrapped her legs around his waist to keep their lower bodies tight. The move paid off, because every step he took jostled her unguarded sex against the jutting curve of his cock.

How much did it cost to dry-clean a pair of men's dress pants? Many more steps and one of them seemed likely to find out. So be it. She wiggled and shifted and did everything in her power to maximize the haphazard caress.

A compass in her head warned her they weren't on the right trajectory to end up at her sofa, but she was too busy being devoured by his fast, hungry mouth to offer directions. Second by second, that mouth grew less controlled. Less accurate. Teeth scraped flesh. His five o'clock shadow scratched across the delicate, kiss-dampened skin around her lips, and made every other patch of damp, delicate skin on her body tingle.

He finally stopped, and let her slide down his body. Even with her eyes closed, she could tell they no longer stood in any of the well-lit areas of her apartment, which meant only one thing. He'd opted for the bedroom. Not that big a deal, normally, but tonight her heart stuttered at the prospect.

Her bedroom contained soft, whimsical flourishes she'd lacked growing up. Booker's trained eyes wouldn't miss the hand-gathered sand dollar collection on her windowsill, or the framed watercolor of Nido Beach at sunrise she'd painted in seventh grade, and definitely not the impractically large, unapologetically romantic iron bed taking up the better part of the room. Granted, she'd just allowed the man unrestricted access to her body, but revealing her romantic, impractical side to him suddenly seemed too intimate.

She opened her eyes and drew back to suggest someplace else. Anywhere. The bathroom, the kitchen, her postage-stamp-sized patio—but just as she started to speak, Booker reached an arm behind his head and yanked his sweater off in one smooth, muscle-rippling move.

The power of speech fled. All she could do was stand and behold. Light from the hallway outlined serve-and-protect shoulders. The slant of sturdy collarbones drew her eye to the chiseled line bisecting his muscled chest. Her gaze slid down, bouncing over each gently rounded slope of his abs, and lingering in every shadowy slash between. Wedges of muscle carved in at his hips and disappeared under the band of white visible above the waist of his undone pants.

Her attention homed in on the ridge…the proud, thick ridge rising from his half-opened fly, and stretching the flap of his boxer briefs. *Hello, sheriff.*

Hair-trigger muscles inside her clenched, even as every self-preserving instinct warned her to back away. Claim an urgent commitment first thing in the morning and get him out the door, pronto, because the stakes tonight suddenly seemed much higher than she could afford. But no amount of willpower could keep her hands from following the path her eyes had traveled.

By the time her fingers snagged in the waistband of his underwear, her hormones had conducted crisis-level negotiations with her self-preserving instincts, and struck a bargain. One teensy ground rule she'd keep to herself. Namely, she could ride him like a wave, until they both crashed and broke, but she would absolutely, positively not let him into her bed. No, sir. When she crawled under the covers at night, she didn't need memories of Booker in there with her.

Luckily, the room offered other options, and a myriad of erotic possibilities flashed through her mind. Pinned between the plaster and Booker's body, digging her heels into his calves as he nailed her to the wall? Bent over her sturdy, antiqued white dresser, watching him in the mirror and holding on for dear life while he rocked her up onto her toes with every thrust? Or maybe...her attention slid to the far corner of her room...something new? She hooked her finger into his belt loop and tugged him over to the chaise she'd splurged on for Christmas because she couldn't resist its sensuous lines.

"Fuck, that's sexy."

"I know." She stroked the white velvet covering the rolled arm of the chaise—another nod to the impractical and romantic. Nothing to do at this point but own it. "A little Christmas gift from me, to me."

He hauled her against him, and snuggled her there in the harbor of big body. "I meant you, walking across the room wearing nothing but high heels, soft light, and the whisker burn I left on your ass."

His words flowed into her ear, and tickled down her spine, finding weak points along the way. What else should she call those parts of her that went soft in response to an unexpected compliment?

This is not a seduction, for Christ's sake, it's a hookup—a long overdue one, born out of simple but persistent physical attraction.

Right, and the sooner she focused on the physical, the easier it would be to remember what tonight was all about. She wriggled out of his grasp, and sat on the chaise.

The velvet felt cool against her backside, and she realized he was right. His teeth or his scratchy jaw had left her a little tender. The slight sting shimmered along receptors in her skin, transmitting the sensation directly to her clit. Or maybe the reaction was some primitive response to the notion that Booker had left his mark on her. Would being with him tonight leave other marks? Marks invisible to the eye, but potentially more permanent?

A stain on your soul…

Her soul had stood up to worse than Ethan Booker. She leaned in and pressed a kiss to the pale strip of skin just above his boxer briefs.

"Wait," he said, and started to take a step away.

Ah, sweet revenge. She reclaimed his belt loops and stopped his retreat. "Close your eyes, say a prayer—whatever you need to do—but don't you dare hold anything back from me."

The corner of his mouth quirked. Deliberately, he took the step back and toed off one shoe. Then the other. "Try to have a little patience, Jailbait. There's a two hundred pound man attached to that cock you've got your eye on, and I sincerely doubt you want me tangled in my pants."

Damn.

He pulled his belt off. The friction of the strap sliding over her knuckles heated her skin. Then he rolled the length, and gave it a toss. It landed on her bed with a small slap. The sound, combined with the sight of stark, masculine accessory made her insides quiver. Silence hung in the room, and she belatedly realized he waited for her to let go of him. When she did, he dipped his head and shucked his pants and underwear off, but not before she saw the flash of his teeth.

All right, another point to him. But starting now, the tables would turn. He wasn't the only one with skills. She knew a few tricks. Once she busted out the practiced and perfected techniques that never failed to get a standing O, she'd have him begging for merc…

Mercy. Nature had been generous with Ethan Booker. She couldn't help staring as he straightened, then scooting to the edge of the seat when he wrapped his hand around the thickest part of his shaft and dragged his fist toward the head, pulling hard enough to lift his balls. "Think you can handle me, Lauralie?"

Yes...no. Maybe. While her hormones, her self-preserving instincts, and some part of her she refused to identify offered conflicting answers, the never-back-down rebel inside her stood up, and grabbed the mic. "What you need to ask yourself, Booker, is how much *you* can handle."

To her surprise, he laughed. She reached for him, but he caught her mid-grab, and wove their fingers together. "At this moment? Not much." He tipped her chin with his other hand, and traced her upper lip with his thumb. "How badly do you need to do this right now?"

Badly, came the humbling response. She usually considered this a treat offered up for the benefit of her partner, with her takeaway being the satisfaction of wielding the power. But not tonight. Tonight she wanted this for her own selfish reasons—to stretch her lips around him, flatten her tongue against his hard, vein-ribbed shaft, and taste him from base to tip.

He manhandled his cock until the head pointed her way. Her tongue crept to the front of her mouth. She licked her lips, parted them, and started to close the distance between them.

"Uh-uh. Don't move. Wait for it."

The unexpected instructions actually made her pause for a moment. "I'm not a patient woman."

He pulled his length out of her reach. "Do we need to skip this after all?"

The bastard. She counted to ten, and then shook her head. "No."

"Good. I'm impatient, too. But tonight's been years in the making, and we're going to do it right"—he gave his cock another stroke, as if he knew watching him handle himself frustrated and aroused her at the same time—"which means I can't let you finish me off with your talented mouth. Cooperate, Lauralie, so I can take care of you. You won't be sorry."

Oh, she might be sorry. Something told her she might be very sorry in a way completely unrelated to sex if she let Booker take care of her, but denying herself now was out of the question. She tucked her hands under her legs, licked her lips, and opened her mouth.

He ran his thumb along the corner of her jaw. "Wider."

An inner voice protested again. The idea of sitting before him, naked and waiting, with her mouth open and exposed to his watchful gaze felt unreasonably vulnerable. But refusing would only reveal the vulnerability to him. She'd walked into this game of chicken with her eyes open and she refused to blink first. Which left only one option.

She complied.

As if he understood what it cost her, he ran his fingers through her hair, brushing it back from her face. "Good girl. I wish you could see what you look like right now, sitting on that virginal white couch, naked and panting, with your lips wet, and your mouth open, ready to receive me. It's a miracle I don't come where I stand."

To distract herself from the heat creeping up her chest, she gripped the cushion and readied for a thrust. Instead, he traced her lips, gliding the smooth, broad head over them. Glossing them.

"Jesus, you have the softest lips. I could spend hours on them."

No, he couldn't, because she'd die. A hungry sound escaped her throat. She dipped her chin and bobbed for him.

Either he failed to anticipate the move, or he took pity on her, but however it happened, she finally had him in her mouth. He slid one hand into her hair, and cupped the other under her chin, constraining her in an unnervingly tender hold. His dark eyes locked on hers for a long moment—long enough for her to struggle with an urge to close hers in case he could see into every corner of her mind—before they dropped to where she held him in her mouth. Pressure mounted in her chest. She dug her fingers into the cushion to ground herself, because a lightheaded sensation rushed her. What the hell had she gotten herself into?

As if he sensed her rising panic, he pushed deeper. The breath she was holding gusted out through her nose. Reflexes kicked in, and she inhaled a mix of oxygen and testosterone.

The quick drag of air steadied her. Confidence returned. *You know exactly what you've gotten yourself into.* Leaning forward, she offered him her whole mouth. Her throat. Everything he could possibly want. The tip of her tongue found a vein along the underside of his shaft and traced the raised path as far as she could, then she sealed her lips tight around his length as she slowly retreated, using enough suction to guarantee he'd feel the pull for days. Thanks to the angle he forced on himself, she could look up and watch his eyes roll back in his head.

So much for his big plans. Another few seconds, and she'd not just finish him off, she'd level him. A minute after that, he'd be tugging his clothes on and making a beeline out her door.

She brushed aside an unfamiliar emptiness at the thought, and got to work, taking him as deep as she could, gorging on his scent, his taste, the leashed power of his thrusts. Fingers dug into her hair. The hand at her throat tightened. She recognized the signs. He was about to become a slave to instinct, and she was about to become a means to an end.

Sure enough, he pumped his hips faster. Just as she prepared for a hot bath at the back of her throat, he did something unprecedented. He dragged his cock out, and hauled her to her feet. "Enough. On the bed. Now."

Every stunned muscle in her body leaped to obey, but what passed for her better judgment issued a reminder. *Not in your bed.*

"Why be so conventional?" She crawled onto the chaise, held onto the lavishly scrolled arm, and arched her back to enhance the pose. "I've got this virginal white sofa just waiting to be…used."

He ran his hands over her, from shoulders to hips, and then ended the caress with a quick slap to her ass. "Next time. Tonight, we need the bed."

There it was again. The assumption they'd do this again. Before she could correct him, he leaned close and added, "What's the matter, Jailbait? Did you lie about no ground rules? Is your bed out-of-bounds?"

The way he saw into her head was out-of-bounds. Her mind now advised her to abort. Eject herself out of this situation because she didn't have the upper hand with Booker, and when it came to sex, she *always* had the upper hand. The rest of her wasn't hearing it though. He'd stood her nose to the wall like a naughty schoolgirl and punished her with an orgasm so brutal it left her shaking. And he hadn't even used his dick on her yet. Her body craved it. Clamored for it. *Okay. Fine. Rule clarification.* You *can be on the bed, just not him.* "Merely trying to keep things interesting."

His smile suggested he didn't buy her explanation. She started to ease off the chaise, but he lifted her and put her on her feet. "Keep trying." He cocked his head. "The bed."

She turned on less than steady legs and walked to the other side of the room, feeling the weight of his stare on her the entire time. Once there, she planted her feet hip's distance apart, bent from the waist, and rested her forearms on the bed. "I trust this is interesting enough for you?"

His footsteps fueled her adrenalin. She lowered her head to the mattress, and lifted onto her toes.

"It's definitely a start. Hand me my belt."

She raised her head as a hundred imaginary feathers fluttered down her spine. "Your…what?"

"My belt," he repeated. "It's right beside you."

"Why?"

"Give it to me, and you'll find out."

If she wasn't in the mood for this, all she had to do was say so. Booker would let it go, without question. Even knowing this, backing down felt too much like surrender. She handed the strap to him, but couldn't help adding a caustic comment. "Who would have guessed there were fifty shades of Sheriff Booker?"

His soft laugh stirred invisible molecules in the air around her. "I would never do anything so *conventional*. Besides"— he folded the belt in half and ran the edge along the back of her thigh—"I think you secretly prefer gentle."

"I told you before, you don't have to be gentle with me."

"You're tough, huh?" The edge of the belt tickled her skin again.

She faced front and held her position. "That's right." Dammit, she was her own worst enemy.

"Okay, tough girl. Be still."

Impossible, because her legs were shaking again. Then he moved, and she sensed more than saw him kneel behind her. *What the…?* She straightened her arms and pushed up as he slid something through the ankle strap of her sandal.

"What are you doing?"

"I told you I had plans for these shoes." Expertly, he threaded the belt through the other strap, nudged the prong into the hole that afforded her the least amount of leeway, and pulled the end through the loop. After a final tug he stood, flipped her around, and dropped her on the bed.

Getting tossed about at his whim shouldn't have excited her, but it did. So did watching him tear open a condom and roll it down his length, but excited or not, she couldn't help challenging the limits of the leather. The impromptu bondage only allowed her to part her ankles a foot, at best. "Nice job, Booker. You rig a hell of a chastity belt."

In answer, he crawled onto the bed. *Illegal move!* Her inner referee cried foul, but all thoughts of calling him out fled as he wrapped his hands around her ankles and lifted her legs, moving into the space left behind as he slowly folded her body in half. His brow winged up and he tossed her words back at her. "Just trying to keep things interesting."

With her knees shoved up to her shoulders and her toes pointed toward the ceiling, her interest was impossible to disguise. He squeezed her butt, and then trailed his fingers into the divide.

Her breath hitched as fingertips cruised over territory his tongue had exploited earlier. "Interested, Lauralie? Or would this violate one of those rules you didn't feel the need to discuss?"

This usually went into the same category as blowjobs, for her. Something she did on occasion, mainly for her partner's satisfaction. Tonight, though, the idea of being filled by Booker in every possible way created a need so profound it bordered on terrifying. When he dropped his gaze to where he touched her, the muscles enduring the patient weight of his fingers quivered. She'd demanded filthy dirty, but now that they were getting down to it, she couldn't find her voice to respond either way.

Maybe he sensed her struggle, because he looked at her again, and said the two words guaranteed to draw a response from her. "Next time."

She reached up and wrapped her fingers around the lowest bar in her headboard. "I'm not big on 'next time,' Booker. Whatever's on your to-do list, you ought to get it done tonight."

"We'll have a next time." The utter certainty in his voice tripped up her pulse. "And a time after that, and then another thousand next times. You want to know why?" He slid his fingers into her heat, and she nearly levitated.

"W-why?"

"Because I've got a thousand ways to please you. You're going to get addicted to the way I make you come. You already are, and I haven't even been inside you yet."

"I'm not."

Those diabolical fingers inched up, spreading her open to his view. "Maybe I'll suck the orgasm out of you, and save being inside you for next time." He grazed the very tip of her clit and turned her into a raw, exposed bundle of need.

"Oh, God. Don't you dare!" She tried to close her legs, but his shoulders prevented her. She'd shatter if he put his mouth on her, but it would be too fast. Too fleeting. A deeper, more elusive orgasm lurked inside her, rare and restive, and slowly building, but she'd never reach it without the help of his long, thick cock.

"No?" He leaned forward, bringing their faces closer, pressing her to the mattress with his weight. "What is it you want?"

Was it possible to die of frustration? "Booker, you know damn well what I want."

He worked his arm between their bodies and dragged the smooth, wide head of his erection through her center. Then he stilled. "Say it. Say you want me."

I want you to shut up and fuck me. She swallowed the reply, in part because it wasn't completely true, but mainly because he might be contrary enough to withhold relief until her side of the conversation satisfied him. She closed her eyes and offered up. "I want you." The admission came out soft, and far too heartfelt. Pride made her tack on, "I want your cock."

He lined them up, head flush against her clit. "When do I put my mouth here?"

She gripped her headboard so tight her knuckles ached, but the need mounted to unbearable proportions—the kind of proportions that rolled right over defenses like pride. Fuck it, she was going to say what he wanted to hear, and they both knew it. "Next time."

He rewarded her reluctant response with a precise surge of his hips, stopping halfway, forcing her body to submit by degrees to the very part of him she'd begged for. His pupils momentarily disappeared behind eyelids suddenly battling gravity, and an irrationally attractive flush rose in his tanned cheeks. He jerked his head back, breathed deeply—in and out—and then refocused on her. "I couldn't hear you. Look me in the eyes and say it louder." Perspiration dampened his face, and a muscle ticked in his jaw, but otherwise, he stayed stubbornly still.

Stranded on a razor thin edge between pleasure and panic, her lips rushed to form the words. "Next time. Next time. Please, Booker…next time." It didn't matter. She wasn't going to survive *this* time. Every part of her felt hot and tight. Her brain in her skull. Her skin. The stretched-to-capacity muscles straining to take him. Her breath turned choppy from the effort. She couldn't move, but she couldn't keep still.

He grabbed the rail above her head, his hands on either side of hers, and withdrew a fraction of an inch.

A sound very close to a sob snuck out between her clenched teeth.

"Are you ready, Lauralie?"

She rocked her hips. A quick, awkward, and mostly

ineffective motion, but enough to have him tip his head back and groan. Then he surged forward.

The powerful thrust sent the bedframe crashing into the wall, and forced a sharp cry out of her. Her legs had nowhere to go except over his shoulders, knees splayed to give him room. His sweat-slicked chest flexed. Muscles rippled in his shoulders, and his abs pulled taut. At the same moment, something inside her loosened a critical fraction. Pleasure seeped into those tight spaces.

And then he started to move.

Calm, cool Ethan Booker had a reputation for self-control, but none of his legendary control came into play now. She belatedly appreciated the extended foreplay he'd subjected her to, because the man fucked without restraint, and he'd primed her so thoroughly she didn't need any.

Fortunate, since the belt binding her ankles and the impossible angle he had her in left her little more than a passenger on this ride. She struggled to hold her position—hips lifted, thighs as wide as possible—because every time he thrust, the base of his cock crushed her clit, pumping pleasure into her bloodstream like a drug.

Over the squeak of her ancient bedsprings, and the smack of flesh, she heard his voice. "Look at me."

She forced her attention from the view of his abs framed by the *V* of her thighs. His tense jaw, and the feverish slashes of color riding high on his cheekbones told her he was close. Dark, intense eyes lured hers.

"Next time, Lauralie. Next time, you'll come on my tongue. Right before I drape you over that pristine white sofa myself, and fuck you until we break the damn thing, but this first time, I want to see your face." He surged deeper, reaching a place inside her where fear and excitement dwelled in a precarious balance, and stirring the unstable mix into something even more volatile.

"Next time," he growled, and thrust again. The words thundered in her ears. Pleasure brutalized her, first coming in waves so rapid and overwhelming they pounded her like a singular force, holding her under, denying her a chance to breathe. Slowly they separated, refining into distinct experiences she could ride out—crests that lifted her to dizzying peaks, followed by shallow valleys of recovery time—and then those eventually subsided and left her floating, warm and safely anchored by the weight of Booker's body. At some point her brain surfaced, and the self-preserving part started in on her.

One lousy rule, and you broke it.

Her satisfied hormones didn't give a single shit. *It was a dumb rule.*

Maybe, but lying here feeling safe and anchored is dumb, too. Wish him a happy New Year, and say good—

He shifted, leaving her cold and startlingly bereft. A moment later, careful fingers undid the strap at her ankle, and slid her sandal off. It landed with a *thump* on her rug while he moved on to the other foot dangling limply over his shoulder. An instant later a second *thump* sounded. "I like the shoes, but they served their purpose."

The same could be said for her, and she'd been happy to serve, but she'd reaped more than her fair share of rewards. The gentlemanly behavior wasn't necessary. She forced her eyes open and raised her head. "I'm sure you have early plans"—his thumb took a slow sweep along her arch— "tomorro…ooohhh."

"Feel good?" His other thumb followed, at the same time his lips found two small, old scars just above her ankle. She started to push herself up, but then he gently swiveled her ankle, taking it through the full range of motion.

Her neck gave out and her head sank back into the pillow. Good? It's possible he'd just given her the third out-of-body experience of the night. "Yuh."

"But I interrupted you." He moved on to her other foot. "You were saying?" he prompted as he eased his fingers between her toes and slowly flexed them forward, and back.

"I was saying"—the scrape of teeth along her instep scattered her thoughts—"I...can't...remember."

"Roll over, so I can do this right." He phrased it almost like a request, even though he was already shifting her onto her stomach.

She let him put her where he wanted her, moaning her gratitude when his thumb pressed its way from her big toe to the back of her knee.

"Lauralie?"

"Hmm?"

His thumbs slid up the center of her thigh, and heat licked into parts of her she could have sworn were too exhausted to respond. "The only plans I have for the next several hours involve you."

Revised rule. He can be in your bed. He can massage any part of you he chooses, with his hands, his mouth, and his very talented dick. But as soon as it's done, he leaves. You absolutely, positively cannot spend the night wrapped in Ethan Booker's arms.

Chapter Four

Laurie blinked herself awake and focused on the glowing red face of the clock on her night table. Quarter 'til five. The one morning she could sleep in, but something had pulled her out of dreamland. A noise, or—

A muscle-corded arm settled across her waist, and a big hand rested along the sensitive skin below her navel. Long fingers extended perilously close to territory they'd exploited repeatedly. That territory swelled and dampened with frightening eagerness at the prospect of being exploited again, but the even breaths fanning her shoulder told her the man responsible for the reaction could literally pull it out of her in his sleep.

The bargain she made with herself last night came back to haunt her. *You absolutely, positively cannot spend the night wrapped in Ethan Booker's arms.*

If you get up now, technically, you haven't broken your rule.

True, and yet…the thought trailed off as Booker shifted again. Something hot and hard jutted into the gap between her thighs. Mmm. So he spent the night? What was the big deal? She had her shit together. She had nothing to hide.

Booker's masterful cock slid a little higher.

Since when have you cared about following rules? Just as she prepared to roll over and break all kinds of rules, she caught movement through the sheer white curtains covering the sliding door that led to her little patio. Seconds later someone bumped into the glass. A muffled snicker followed, and Laurie's stomach sank. She knew that laugh.

Happy fucking New Year. She slipped out of bed fast, and silently crossed the room, biting back a groan as sore muscles in exceedingly personal places complained about the sudden call to action. The curtain provided minimum protection for her modesty, but she drew it back far enough to glare through the glass and stop the woman on the other side from knocking.

Good old mom. Here for a surprise five a.m. visit after — what had it been this time — a year and a half of blissful absence? She looked like shit. Two inches of grown-out, dirty-blond roots contrasted with brassy red. Black liner ringed her over-bright eyes, and her tight, low-cut dress in an extremely unbefitting white showed signs of a few spilled drinks. Chapped lips pulled into an artificial smile, and she waved enthusiastically before opening her mouth to speak.

Laurie shook her head, and pressed a finger to her lips. Loaded or not, Denise got the message. She made a zipping motion across her mouth and tossed the imaginary key over her shoulder.

Hilarious. Laurie held up her hand and mimed, *Five minutes.* Then she pointed to the left, silently telling her mother to go around front. Denise nodded, executed an unsteady pivot, and meandered off the patio, leaving the wooden gate hanging open. Laurie let the curtain fall back into place as soon as her mother disappeared from view.

Five minutes. A quick glance at the bed confirmed

Booker remained asleep. Maybe there was a patron saint of put upon daughters because the third drawer of her dresser barely made a noise as she carefully slid it open. She stepped into a faded pair of cut-offs, breathing in as denim dragged over newly sensitive skin. Her eyes tried to drift to the cause of the tender spots, but she denied the detour by pulling on a white hoodie with Babycakes' trademark—a silhouette of a pinup girl wearing a short, frilly apron and holding a cake— emblazoned across the front in periwinkle blue. Calling herself dressed, she headed to the door. Halfway out of the room, however, her eyes won the tug-of-war. She paused and looked back at the bed.

Booker had rolled into the space she'd vacated, and lay stretched out on his stomach with his dark, rumpled head nestled in her pillow. A massive shoulder blocked the lower half of his face, but the long, tapered lines of his back remained on display—all the way down past the dimples at the base of his spine. The comforter covered his hips, but as she watched, a sleepy kick sent the covers to the end of the bed. Then he settled, one knee drawn up toward his elbow, unknowingly treating her to an awe-inspiring view of his ass, the endearingly vulnerable cushion of his balls, and the root of his cock. Under different circumstances, she might have snuck her hand into that unprotected crevice to give him a good morning squeeze before wrapping her fingers around his hard-on and putting it to good use.

But the circumstances right now involved her mother on her doorstep, wanting money for sure, and likely to wake the whole neighborhood if Laurie didn't get out there and manage the situation. She started to walk away, but…dammit. Even as the two-minute warning bell rang in her mind she hurried to the bed, soundlessly opened her nightstand drawer, and withdrew a pen and sticky note. She squandered another quarter of a minute biting her shredded cuticle and trying to figure out what the hell to say. Finally, she scrawled, *Happy New Year, Booker. See you around.*

Lame.

Yeah, well, the whole thing was lame, she acknowledged as she walked through her apartment. Leaving a note for a one-night stand? Lame. Thinking she actually had her shit under control? Lame. Having her mother show up before dawn, stoned or drunk or just plain crazy? Very lame.

The remnants of last night's party littered the kitchen and living room. Glassware and small plates took up every available surface, along with cocktail napkins, noisemakers, and party hats. Confetti and streamers decorated the floor. Picked over trays of food sat out on the counter separating the two rooms—some of Babycake's trademark mini-cakes, but also a selection of flatbreads and canapés. She'd wanted to remind people she could do more than sweets, and judging by the meager leftovers, she'd succeeded. She picked her way through the mess and opened the hallway closet where she kept her flip-flops and purse. The hinge squeaked when she opened it. She froze, and listened.

Nothing stirred in the apartment as far as she could tell. Relieved, she shoved her feet into the flip-flops and grabbed her purse. Drawing a fortifying breath, she pulled the front door open, stepped out, and quickly closed it behind her. No point giving the woman any ideas about coming inside for a visit.

"Lauralie! Happy New Year, baby!"

The staggering embrace accompanying the loud greeting nearly knocked her off her feet. She struggled for balance and breathed through a surge of nausea brought on by sour breath and sharp angles of a body too accustomed to a liquid diet. "Denise, it's five in the morning. Keep your voice down."

"Right. Sorry. Shhh... Don't want to wake your company."

"I don't want to wake my neighbors. What are you doing here?"

"Why, sweetheart." She pressed her hand to a still ample chest, though it looked to be getting some help from a push-up bra these days. "I came to see you. Who's the lucky guy? Anyone I know?"

Oh, hell no. They were not indulging in girl talk. There's be no stopping Mommy Dearest if she thought her daughter offered an in with a man of Booker's resources. "No one special." The words tasted bitter in her mouth. She set off down the walkway, toward her carport at the back of the white stucco and red-tile-roofed building. Montenido boasted newer, grander examples of Southern California Mediterranean architecture, but she liked the classic 1930's style of the small complex, not to mention the comparative affordability of the rent. "What do you want?"

"To see my baby girl, silly. I've missed you." The *clomp-clomp* of narrow heels against concrete confirmed Denise followed. While Laurie fished her keys from the inner pocket of her purse, she looked down at the silver sandals strapped to her mom's feet. Yikes. The sandals bore an uncanny resemblance to the ones she'd worn last night. An old saying about apples and trees sprang to mind—insulting when applied to her—and she made a mental note to get rid of the blasted shoes. They hurt her feet anyway.

Booker knows a cure for aching feet. Remember?

Yeah, well, fun was fun, but she couldn't rely on Booker to save her from the uncomfortable aftereffects of every questionable decision. Though he'd done so more than once in the past ten years. She preferred to stand on her own two feet, and tacky silver sandals didn't advance that goal.

"Mission accomplished. You've seen me." She stopped at the bumper of her new black Ford Expedition. New to her, at any rate. She'd needed something bigger and more reliable than her old Explorer for deliveries and had negotiated an end-of-year discount on a certified pre-owned model, fresh off a four-year lease. Between upgrading her vehicle and the bonuses she'd paid to her employees, she'd drained the little cushion in her finances, but she considered both expenses an investment in her business. She also had six grand in custom cake deposits sitting in her safe at the bakery. April, May, and June were busy wedding months in Montenido and thanks to some favorable write-ups and good word-of-mouth, her upstart little bakery had nabbed half a dozen large orders. She tapped the unlock button on her key, and then activated the power liftgate. The beep echoed in the cool morning air, but the trunk door lifted almost soundlessly.

"Lauralie, don't be so freaking literal. I meant talk to you. Catch up. Nice car. Is it new?"

She ignored the question and walked between the SUV and the wall until she reached the rack at the back of the carport where she and a few of her neighbors stored their surfboards. A three-digit combination unlocked the rack. She slid her board out, re-locked the rack, and walked back to the SUV. Denise jumped out of the way when she swung the board around and loaded it into the trunk alongside her wetsuit and a straw tote containing her bikini and towel. "I'm headed out, and I won't be back for hours." A press of a button shut the truck. If only she could shut Denise out as easily, but the woman specialized in difficult. Turning, she faced her mother. "If there's a point to your visit, now would be a good time to get to it."

"I need a teensy loan."

"No." She straightened, mentally kicking herself, because even though she'd seen the request for money coming a mile away, some stupid part of her had secretly hoped Denise had come to apologize for being such a shitty mother, and—what the hell, as long as she was dreaming—maybe give *her* something for a change.

"Have some compassion for your mother. I need a

little help, and I don't think it's too much to expect my own daughter to be there for me."

"Just like you've been there for me?"

"I did the best I could by you. I was gone a lot on account of my career. I didn't have the luxury of hanging around the house all day taking care of a kid."

What career? Denise had been a "personal assistant" to an endless string of guys who wanted to fuck her, invariably did, and then walked away when they realized no fuck was worth the accompanying drama. She walked to the driver's side and yanked the door open. "I can't take care of an adult. Sorry."

"But you're doing so well. You can afford this big, shiny car. I think you can afford to give me a loan to remove a tumor from my uterus."

"You know, I could have sworn I gave you money for a hysterectomy three years ago."

Denise blushed, though it could have been a sign of temper rather than shame. "That doctor was a quack. He didn't know what he was doing, and now I'm paying for his incompetence. I've talked to a lawyer about suing his thieving ass, but it costs money to file a lawsuit."

"You've come to the wrong place. I don't have any cash to spare." With that, she hauled herself into the driver's seat.

Denise skittered over, nimble as a spider, and stuck her face into Laurie's. "You selfish brat. Don't bullshit me. I know all about your fancy bakery. I saw a glossy spread in *Montenido Magazine*, gushing about how all the rich suckers around here stand in line to plunk down five dollars for a cinnamon bun or fifty bucks for a dozen cupcakes. Not your best picture, by the way, but Jesus Christ—fifty bucks for cupcakes? You're raking it in. If you turn me away, I'm going to have no choice but to camp outside that little business of yours and explain to everyone who passes how you can't spare a dime for your own mother in her hour of need. A few of them might decide to help a fellow human rather than buy a treat. Who knows?"

Threats were also to be expected. 'Help me, or you can kiss your precious spot on the surf team good-bye.' 'Help me, or I'll come down to your job and have a word with your boss.' And they weren't empty threats. Denise would do whatever it took. The only difference now was Laurie had more to lose than an extra-curricular activity, or a minimum wage paycheck. This time, it was her livelihood at stake. She knew better than to waste her breath on the realities of owning a small business. Her mother didn't give a shit about reality.

She also knew better than to meet the threat with anything except threats of her own—not initially, at least. "If you panhandle outside my shop, I'll call the cops and have you removed."

"Which gives *Montenido Magazine* an interesting follow-up story. 'Successful Business Owner Has Ailing Mother Arrested.' That'll bump the readership."

"You're overestimating people's interest." But she wasn't. People couldn't look away from a train wreck. Denise ruined everything she touched, including her daughter, and if she touched Babycakes, Laurie had no doubt she would ruin it, too.

"Why bring us to that? Cough up fifteen thousand dollars, cash, and nothing turns ugly. I catch the next train to LA and see to myself."

Fifteen *thousand*? All she could do was laugh at the outrageous demand. "Are you high? I don't have fifteen grand sitting around, and even if I did I couldn't get to it on New Year's Day." Still, her mother's proposition gave her hope. She wanted a quick score. Much larger than what she usually tried to bleed out of her daughter, but there was a number that would get the woman out of her life. Today. They just had to arrive at the figure.

Sure enough, Denise folded her arms and jutted her chin. "How much can you get right now?"

"I have forty, maybe fifty bucks in my wallet."

"Stop fucking with me. You've got an ATM card."

"And a daily limit."

"Fine. If that's how you want to play it, give me a thousand today, and I'll settle for ten grand first thing Monday. I'll come to the bakery. Have it ready for me."

Abso-fucking-lutely not, but at least now they had a realistic ballpark. A door slammed somewhere in the complex, and a panicked desperation fueled her counter-offer. "I've got six thousand in the safe at the bakery. I'll take you over there right now, and give you every cent, provided you get the hell out of Montenido this morning. Best and final offer. You've got five seconds to make up your mind."

"I'll need a ride to the train station."

Somehow, she resisted the urge to slap the triumphant smirk off her mother's face. "Done. Get in."

While Denise scurried around the front of the SUV, Laurie revved the engine to life and promised herself a long, soul-cleansing surf session as soon as she dumped her mother at the train station. Getting blackmailed by a blood relative only hours into the New Year effectively sucked away the orgasmic glow left over from last night's amazing, but inadvisable, hookup with Booker. Thank God he hadn't woken. The only thing more humiliating than caving to her mother's threats would be Booker witnessing it. The fearless visage she strived to maintain would disappear in the blink of an eye, and she didn't think she could handle the loss—not when it came to him.

Denise hoisted her bony frame into the passenger seat, and slammed the door. "Got anything to drink in that bakery of yours, Lauralie? I feel like celebrating."

Congratulations. Your New Year can't get any worse.

Chapter Five

Alone. Booker didn't need to open his eyes to confirm what all his other senses told him. Scents of champagne, vanilla, and sex lingered on the sheets, but no sleep-warmed curves pressed against him. No rustle of movement from the kitchen or bathroom disturbed the silence. He wasn't just alone in the bed. He was alone in the whole damn apartment.

He scrubbed a hand over his eyes and blinked them open. Watery light filtered into the bedroom through the filmy drapes. Yep. Alone. Maybe she'd run to the store for coffee filters, or, better yet, condoms? A yellow Post-it note on the nightstand flagged his attention. He sat up, and peeled it off the white-painted wood.

Happy New Year, Booker. See you around.

Frustration leaked out in the form of a sigh. Leave it to her to try and turn them into a one-night stand. *Sorry, Jailbait. Not going to make it that easy for you.* He crumpled the note and chucked it at the small wastebasket beside the dresser. It hit the rim and bounced onto the rug. Fuck. Apparently nothing would be easy this morning.

He swung his legs to the floor, but before he could reach down and retrieve the note now littering her rug, his phone rang. His do not disturb settings left only one possible caller. Dispatch. Changing course, he snagged his pants, and dug the phone from his pocket. While he was at it, he slid hers from the other pocket and placed the slim, white device on the dresser. Had she forgotten he had it, or had she simply been too busy bolting to pause for electronics?

Phone abandonment—the human equivalent of gnawing off a limb to escape a trap.

Suppressing another sigh, he flicked his thumb across the screen of his phone. "Booker."

The dispatch supervisor's voice flowed over the line. "Sorry to hit you on your day off, Sheriff, but we've got a less than happy New Year underway, and Chief Nelson asked us to make you aware."

Chief Nelson headed the fire department. Booker used his shoulder to hold the phone to his ear and dragged his pants on. "What's happening, Michelle?"

"Structure fire at Nido Point Plaza. It's the little shopping center on the southwest corner of—"

"I know it." A jolt of adrenalin charged his system. Babycakes occupied a storefront at one end of the plaza. Lauralie "Anyone inside? Any injuries?"

"Yet to be determined. According to witness reports, the entire east wall of the building is engulfed. FD's on the way."

"So am I." He felt for his keys, but then remembered he didn't have them...or his car. "Shit. I need a ride. Send a unit for me." He rattled off the address.

"Will do."

"Thanks. Call me if you get any new information." He disconnected, yanked his sweater over his head, and then scanned the floor for his shoes. Lauralie might well be in that building, and here he was, miles away, with no car, no radio, wearing last night's clothes, and...fuck...in possession of her phone. He grabbed it, shoved his feet into his shoes and sprinted out the door. Dammit, when he got his hands on her, he was going to—he didn't even know. At this point he couldn't think past finding her.

Desperation sent him around the building to the carports, in the hopes of seeing her car, but her slot sat empty. He jogged to the front, dialed dispatch, and waited, helplessly, while nightmare scenarios played through his mind.

The supervisor picked up. "What do you need?"

"Do you have eyes on the fire?"

"Yep."

"Any vehicles in the parking lot? A black Ford Expedition?"

"Hold on."

While he held, a cruiser approached the complex. Booker raised a hand to catch the attention of the deputy behind the wheel. Dave Petty nodded back, a late-career member of the department coasting toward retirement—but a capable coast. Dispatch popped back on the line while he slid into the passenger seat. "No vehicles in the parking area. My eyewitnesses can't get a look behind the building without approaching the fire. I've instructed them to stay back. FD's just arrived on the scene, along with two of your units."

"Got it."

He switched to radio, contacted the units, and requested a search for vehicles behind the building. Then he slipped back into helpless waiting mode, and silently told himself she wasn't there. She would have parked in front. She *always* parked in front.

Petty pulled up on the plaza before anyone reported back. Booker leaped out of the cruiser, instinctively cataloging details as he approached the scene—his deputies establishing a perimeter and keeping a growing crowd of onlookers at bay, fire trucks occupying strategic points in the parking lot, and firefighters racing to unfurl hoses. Flames devoured one side of the building. Smoke rolled from the structure in thick, dark clouds. He didn't need a fire science degree to know the blaze originated in the bakery. The first team got a hose on the fire. He headed over, ready to commandeer the damn thing and drag them through the door.

A blaring horn and the screech of brakes whipped his head around. He looked up, and nearly passed out from relief at the sight of Lauralie's black Expedition lurching to a stop by the curb of the street leading to the plaza. An instant later she rushed around the front of the car. Eyes wide and riveted on the fire, she careened down the landscaped slope to the parking lot. He ran toward her, prepared to intercept 110 pounds of frantic woman before she did serious damage to herself.

She lost her footing three quarters of the way down, and started to slide, but he caught her before she tumbled to the asphalt.

The impact of their bodies knocked a gasp out of her. She would have bounced off him and continued running, but he had his arms around her, and locked her to him even as she fought to get free. Giving in to bone-deep relief, he buried his face in her hair. Wet hair, full of sand, salt, and the scent of the ocean. She'd left him asleep in her bed and escaped to go surfing. They'd talk that shit out later, but right now he didn't care. She wasn't inside the bakery, and that's all that mattered.

Her struggles gradually subsided, but her body succumbed to bone-rattling shakes. She said something over and over against his chest. Keeping himself between her and the sight of the burning building, he adjusted his hold to let her raise her head.

Her hoarse, broken words immediately reached him.

"Let me go."

"Not a chance."

"It's mine. I have to see. I have to."

He bundled her over to the cruiser—out of the way of people, equipment, and the worst of the smoke—and put her in the backseat. Then he parked himself by the open door. That's when he realized his back pocket vibrated nonstop. Word traveled fast. He pulled her phone out and handed it to her.

She stared at the glowing screen so long the vibrations stopped, and then she lifted utterly defeated eyes to his. "I can't talk to anybody right now."

A part of him wanted to gather her into his arms, and promise he'd hold the world back, but allowing her to withdraw into her misery didn't do her any favors. She needed support, even if she didn't want to admit it. The buzzing began anew. He held out the phone once more. She wouldn't respond to sympathy—at least not from him—so he resorted to scolding. "You have friends, and right now they're frantic to know you're okay. Don't put them through what I experienced this morning."

Scolding worked. She accepted the phone and answered the call. He listened long enough to assure himself she'd engaged, then he gave her shoulder a squeeze and strode to where one of his deputies stood motioning for him.

The rest of the morning passed in a blur. More onlookers arrived, including most of the bakery employees. His deputies managed the crowd while Nelson's men put down the fire. Walk-throughs confirmed the building had been empty, which was a blessing of the early hour and the holiday. The unit next door to the bakery sustained some damage—mostly smoke and water—but the bakery itself was a total loss.

He was wrapping up a call with the desk deputy at the station when he turned to see Chief Nelson headed toward him, carrying a clipboard and talking to Lauralie.

"…appreciate you giving us your statement."

"I'm sorry I don't have much to tell. Any other morning I'd have been in the kitchen by five-thirty, but we were closed due to the holiday."

Nelson offered the clipboard to Booker. "We'll call that a lucky break, since it means we're dealing with damage to property only, and not people."

Booker skimmed the chief's notes containing the preliminary information for the fire report—which didn't set forth anything he didn't already know—and handed the board back. "Any word on the cause of the fire?"

"Officially? No." Nelson shook his head. "The fire investigator will determine origin and cause, but it will take some time for them to work their magic."

"Unofficially?" Booker pressed because Nelson had been on the job a long time. The guy knew how to read a structure fire.

The older man glanced toward the building. "Based on the thermal pattern on the back wall, I'd say electrical."

"What happens now?" she asked. "Do I get some sort of report from you and submit it to my insurance company, or…?"

"You can get a copy of the incident report in a few days, but don't wait for that. Call your insurer today and give them notice of the claim. Who's your carrier?"

She named the company, and Booker watched a barely perceptible wince tighten Nelson's lips.

"What?" Apparently Lauralie noticed, too.

"I hear they offer competitive rates," the chief said diplomatically.

"That's why I went with them. Please don't tell me they're about to go bankrupt or something, because I need the insurance money to pay back my business loan."

"No, no. They're solvent, as far as I know," Nelson replied, "and it's not my place to rate the carriers…"

"But?"

The man rocked back on his heels and squinted at the sky for a moment. "They're not known for processing claims quickly, and they like their loopholes. You'll want to stay on top of the adjudicator and the investigation. Don't give them any reason to drag things out."

Laurie closed her eyes and groaned. Booker rested his hand along the back of her neck and gently kneaded the tense muscles there.

"Okay. Good to know. I appreciate the tip." She drew in a breath and refocused on Nelson. "I know it's New Year's Day, and I'm not the only case in your investigator's workload, but about how long do you think it will take to complete the investigation?"

"Our investigation? Maybe thirty days, assuming the lab isn't backed up."

"Holy shit. Thirty days, seriously?"

"And that's just *our* investigation. Regardless of our findings, your carrier will conduct a separate investigation. They'll have an independent firm come out and inspect the scene, gather their own evidence, and probably do their own analysis using their own forensic experts. If they identify a product failure or maintenance issue as the cause of the fire, they'll have to notify those parties, and give them the opportunity to inspect the scene too."

"Oh my God. How long is *that* going to take?"

"Stay on top of them," was all Nelson said.

"Great," she murmured, and shoved her fists deep into the front pocket of her hoodie. The tension in the fabric mirrored the tension in her body. Booker watched her chew her lip and do some mental calculations. It didn't take long and her expression told him the answer was a big, fat, *You.*

Are. Fucked. As soon as they were alone, he'd get the specifics and figure out how to help. The trick wasn't coming up with money—he had plenty—the trick was getting her to accept it.

"Can I go in and—"

"No." Booker responded, even though he knew she'd directed the question to Nelson. Protocol prevented anyone except emergency personnel from accessing the scene until the investigators were done, but even more important, he wasn't letting her wander through a burned-out, potentially unstable structure.

Her indignant gaze swung his way, and her hands flew from the pocket of her sweatshirt to her hips. "It's my property in there. I might be able to salvage some things."

Nelson backed him. "I can't allow you inside until the building inspector signs off and my investigators complete their examination of the scene, but if you or your employees have any personal effects in the unit, my crew can retrieve them before we secure the premises."

"All right." She released a pent-up breath, and pushed her hands back into her pocket. "I understand." To Nelson, she said, "I can't think of anything, but let me check with my team. I'll be right back."

"I'll come over in a second," Nelson said. Lauralie nodded, and walked across the lot to where friends and employees had assembled to commiserate and offer support.

He turned to the chief. "Nothing looked suspicious?"

"No. I'm pretty confident it started as an electrical fire. Burn patterns point to a wall outlet. There really shouldn't be much for her insurance company to spin their wheels on, but you know how it goes."

"Yeah. I know her, too, though. She's a fighter."

"Good. For my own selfish reasons, I hope she gets it sorted out and reopens soon. I'm partial to her cinnamon twists. Later."

"Later," Booker echoed. His attention strayed to Lauralie. He wanted to go after her, but Deputy Petty approached and pointed out most of the looky-loos had dispersed now that the fire was out, which was his way of asking to go off the clock. Fair question. It was New Year's Day, after all. Booker checked in with his deputies and worked out the logistics.

While he accomplished the chore, he kept watch over Lauralie. She and her employees congregated at one end of the parking lot, in a small area inside the yellow caution tape, sorting through the few items firefighters pulled from shop. Occasionally she took a call, or stopped to speak with someone who wandered over despite the tape. Through it all she wore her patented I-can-handle-anything look.

Time to wrap this up. Picking through charred remains and putting on a brave face for employees and customers wouldn't rebuild her business any faster. He walked over. She stood with her back to him, listening to a red-faced blond woman who punctuated her rapid-fire speech with air pokes from her extended index finger. He didn't recognize her, but whoever she was, she'd evidently decided the warning tape didn't apply to her, and she clearly hadn't stopped by to offer assistance.

"...bad luck, or your own negligence. Ultimately it's not my problem. *My* problem is you have a thousand dollar deposit on a wedding cake you're not going to be able to deliver. I want my money back, and I want it back now."

He increased his pace, and prepared to call out, because he was ready to boot the blonde for trespassing, but Lauralie responded first.

"You know what, Cindy? I don't walk around with thousand dollar rolls on me. If you check the order form you signed, you'll note I have thirty days from the date you cancel to issue a refund."

The blonde pulled a folded form from her purse, flicked it

open and scanned the page. Then she looked up and glared at Lauralie. "I'm canceling."

Lauralie nodded. "Fine. You'll get your refund within the specified time frame."

The other woman stood for a moment, obviously unsatisfied and seemingly prepared to argue. Then her attention shifted to him. She swallowed, and smoothed a hand over her hair. "I'd better, or I'll see you in court." With that, she stomped off.

Lauralie let out a long breath and pressed the heel of her hand to her forehead. Finally, she turned, and stopped short when she saw him. "You're still here."

"I'm still here. Did you think I'd just sneak off?"

• • •

Her cheeks burned. Yes, she'd snuck off this morning, but, hell, she'd done him a favor. One he'd never know about, if she had her way. Nobody deserved to kick off New Year's Day dealing with her mother. Look what it had done to her. Less than an hour after she'd handed the contents of her safe over to Denise, the place had burned down. Another example of her mother's toxic Karma. Or maybe she was she producing her very own toxic Karma now? Like mother, like daughter.

"I didn't sneak off. I left you a note."

"I can't tell you how comforting that note was to me when I woke up alone in your apartment to the sound of my dispatch supervisor telling me your shop was on fire. I didn't have a fucking clue if you were inside."

Shit. Defensive words sprang to her lips, but she swallowed them down, because the look on his face silenced her. She wasn't so absorbed in her own situation she couldn't put herself in someone else's shoes. "I'm sorry you worried. I'm fine."

Just fine. My business is gone. The people I employ are out of jobs. I owe six thousand dollars in deposit refunds I used to make my mother go away. My insurance sucks, and I'm probably going to default on my business loan. But otherwise? Best New Year ever.

The tension in his jaw relaxed. His shoulders came down a notch. "You're not fine, but you will be."

"Yeah." She meant to sound confident, because she didn't intend to pour out her troubles to anyone, but the single word fell short of the mark to her ears.

"You're tired, and you've done everything you can do for now. Let's go." He held out his hand, palm up. "Give me your keys. I'll drive you home."

Sweet of him to offer, in his I'm-in-charge way, but invisible hooks inside her refused to detach from the charred remains of her livelihood. As painful and illogical as it was to linger in the parking lot, so long as she did, Babycakes existed in her present. Once she left, her dream-come-true officially became part of her past. A memory. Her days wouldn't start with her strolling under the striped awning. No more unlocking the door to the tidy shop, and feeling her chest swell with pride. She couldn't let it go yet, but Booker didn't need to hang out while she mourned. More importantly, she didn't need any witnesses.

"Thanks, but I'm going to try to reach my insurance agent before I leave. Make sure I'm not overlooking anything. I'll see you…" *shit* "…around."

He let the tactless choice of farewells pass without comment, but not the underlying attempt to stand her ground. "Lauralie, it's time to go." He closed his hand around her arm, and gently but firmly guided her toward her car. Out of nowhere a memory rose up, of the same gentle but firm hand guiding her off the beach a lifetime ago, rescuing her from her own bad judgment.

Funny how history repeated itself. Still, she wasn't sixteen anymore, and she took pride in having the strength and smarts to deal with any situation she faced. On her own. She genuinely appreciated peoples' kindness today, and their efforts to help, but she'd sent them away for a reason. Laurie Peterson didn't lean on anyone. She gave out advice. She supplied a shoulder to cry on, not vice versa. Chelsea was the only possible exception, and even their dynamic tended to work the other way.

Fumbling the good-bye to Booker didn't qualify him as the second exception, especially not to confide all the troubles weighing on her now. She needed time alone, all the more so because some weak part of her longed to crawl onto his lap, and bawl her eyes out against his chest while he held her in his arms and told her everything would be okay.

No bawling except in absolute seclusion. Forcing her spine straighter, she dug her keys out of the front pocket of her shorts. "I can drive myself. You must have had plans for today."

"I'm wide open at the moment." He looked around the empty parking lot. "I'm also stranded."

The secluded bawling part of her day just got pushed. She unlocked her truck. "Hop in. I'll give you a lift to your car." It was the least she could do after…everything. She could hold herself together a little longer.

Dark eyes roamed her face, looking for what, she wasn't sure, and even less sure she wanted him to find it. But she couldn't turn away. After a moment, he nodded. "Thanks."

She started the engine, and waited while he got in and buckled his seat belt. His five o'clock shadow from last night was now a full-blown unshaven jaw. His finger-combed hair waved back from his face in the kind of ridiculously attractive disarray that only worked for guys. All the rugged masculinity sent her mind back to this morning, when she'd left him sprawled in her bed. Her system reacted with a violent and inappropriate burst of lust—like an engine backfiring in a funeral procession.

Reassuring how in the midst of a crisis, your hormones remain in full working order. She put the car into gear and pulled away from the curb. The burned-out remains of Babycakes slanted across her rearview mirror, and failure sat like a boulder on her chest. She pushed through the pain to locate her voice. "Where's your car?"

"At my parent's house."

Her foot smashed the brake. "*Where?*"

"I left it there last night." He looked uncharacteristically defensive. "Is that a problem?"

"No." She shook her head, and resumed driving. Not a problem. A reminder. They called the same town home, but Booker and she came from very different worlds. His parents lived in the most coveted part of Montenido. The part she only visited as a member of the hired help. Yes, technically, for a moment there, she'd clawed her way up to business owner, but fate had kicked her back down.

A hand moved her hair behind her shoulder. "Tell me."

"Tell you what?"

"I spent the better part of a decade watching you, and the best parts of last night inside you. The tough-as-nails act you put on for everyone else doesn't work on me. Tell me what you need."

The whole curl-up-on-his-lap-and-cry scenario suddenly threatened to become a mortifying reality. Slippery panic and a desperate need to push him a safe distance from the shit-storm of her life had her responding with a cynical laugh. "I need six grand in the next thirty days. How much can I put you down for?"

"Six grand." His reply came without hesitation.

A scrolled iron gate flanked by carved marble lions passed

on the left. She drove on, steering her SUV up the winding, palm-lined road to the rarified hilltop Montenido's wealthiest families called home. His family included. He didn't choose to live like this, but six thousand wouldn't set him back. Not in the least.

It set *her* back though—to a place she'd sworn she'd never go. Just asking for the money made her exactly like her mother, approaching every person in her life with her hand out and a hard-luck story on her lips. Her mind recoiled from the realization, and struck back with unflattering meanness. "That certainly puts a price on last night."

She braced for anger. Disgust. She had it coming after such an obnoxious comment. But he laughed.

"Yeah, right. If we're charging by the orgasm, *you* owe *me* for last night. I would have let you try to even the score this morning, but you chickened out."

"I didn't chicken out."

"No?"

"I had…reasons…for leaving."

"I checked the surf report. The waves weren't that good."

The quiet disappointment in his voice tempted her to come clean. "My…" Nope. She couldn't do it. God, she sucked. "This is a pointless conversation. I'm not taking your money. I'm not a freaking charity."

"I'm not offering a donation."

She expelled her breath and prepared to cut him off, but he kept talking. "Once you get the bakery running again, you can pay me back. In the meantime, I reduce the amount of time I'm deprived of my morning carbs and coffee."

"I can't take your money as a loan either."

"Why not? I've got some I'm not using."

"Because…" Frustration sent the response tumbling out of her mouth, unfiltered. "You wouldn't understand, because you've never had to worry about money. The stakes in life go down considerably when you have that kind of security. Everything's easier. I don't have the same safety net. I've had to earn every damn thing I've gotten. It's who I am, and what I expect of myself. Right now I have no income, no collateral, and a bunch of debt. I can't qualify for a loan. Taking one from you is just a different brand of bailout."

Without direction, she pulled to the shoulder beside the privacy hedge demarking the perimeter of his parents' property. She'd never been here before, but she knew the Booker family home the same way locals in Hyannis Port knew the Kennedy compound—from a distance, on the other side of gates and walls.

He stared out the passenger window while red rose under his cheekbones and a muscle in his jaw ticked. "Believe it or not, money doesn't buy everything. I've actually had to work for a few things, too."

Great. She'd offended him. He resented implications his family's wealth or connections afforded him advantages, and, in all fairness, he never played the wealth and connections cards to get ahead. Still, they were there, putting him ahead of the game even if he preferred not to leverage them. A sighted person walking around with his eyes closed could tell himself he understood what it was like to be blind, but he didn't. Regardless, the man had stood shoulder-to-shoulder with fire fighters, his deputies, and the rest of the emergency responders, and tried to rescue her business. He deserved respect and she hadn't meant to imply otherwise. "I'm sorry. I just meant—"

"I know what you meant."

His terse reply whipped the air between them, like a battle flag snapping in the wind. After a tense moment of silence, he blew out a tired breath. "Lauralie…" His voice trailed off and he ran his palm over the back of his neck. Booker, tongue-tied? It was adorable and disconcerting at once.

"How about a temporary job?" he finally asked.

The question took her by surprise. She straightened. "My livelihood went down in flames today. If you know of a job, I'm all ears."

"My sister's getting married on Valentine's Day."

"Congratulations. Don't tell me she's waited until now to think about a wedding cake—"

"No." He cleared his throat. "As far as I know, she's got all that handled. The job doesn't involve baking, it involves acting."

Huh? "I don't understand."

"This wedding puts me in an awkward position. I could use your help getting clear of it. I'm willing to pay you for your time."

"Sorry. I'm confused. How does your sister's wedding land you in an awkward position? Do you dislike her fiancé, or something? Hey." A nasty thought formed in her mind and left a queasy suspicion in the pit of her stomach. "Does this acting job involve me hitting on your sister's fiancé so you can expose him as a faithless, gold-digging manwhore?"

"Jesus, no. Nothing like that. Aaron's a great guy. Solid. And if I doubted his motives, I'd have no problem confronting him directly, not resorting to a sting operation."

The queasy feeling faded, but a little envy swept in, flowing toward Booker's sister. What would it be like to have a protective family looking out for her? She'd probably never know. "So, you're…happy for them?"

"Yes, but on a personal level, I'm fucked, because as soon as Kate and Aaron announced their engagement, I became collateral damage."

"How so?"

"My mother convinced herself she engineered their match. She introduced them, and claims credit for finding them their soul mates."

"Aw. That's sweet."

"It's delusional. And terrifying. The woman already believes she knows better than the rest of us how we should live our lives. Now she also thinks she knows who we should live them with."

She couldn't help herself. She laughed. "Okay, so your mom is a busybody with a newfound knack for matchmaking. I don't see how this impacts you. You're not the one walking down the aisle on account of her."

"If she gets her way, I will be. The next match she intends to make is *mine*."

Laughter threatened again, but she managed to hold it in. "What's wrong, Booker, not ready to settle down? You know, I think you should reconsider. I mean, you're well into your mid-thirties now—"

"I'm thirty-*two*," he shot back, "which is early thirties, no matter how you do the math, but certainly old enough to know I don't want or need my mother interfering in my life."

"You poor, poor man. Hey, I have a suggestion. Why don't you grow a pair and tell mommy to mind her own business?" Big words coming from a woman who handled her own mother by paying the woman to get lost. But Booker didn't need to know that. Nobody needed to know that.

He shook his head. "Trying to change her mind once she's locked onto an objective is a waste of breath. She's got me in her sights, like a sniper. Her ego's involved, she's motivated, and for the next six weeks she's got unprecedented opportunity, in the form of a wedding and half a dozen related events I have no option but to attend. Unless I take countermeasures, she'll use each and every one of those occasions to shoot single women at me in rapid-fire succession. My only hope is to take away her reason for pulling the trigger."

"Okay, Sheriff, I'll bite. How do you plan to convince her you're bulletproof?"

"I don't. I take the opposite tactic." He crossed his arms, and smiled a slow, cunning smile that did unspeakable things to her insides. "I show up with a date and make her believe fate beat her to the kill."

Beat her to the...*kill*? This sounded bad. Risky. "Forgive me. I'm not fluent in The Art of War. What, exactly, are you saying?"

"I'll pay you six thousand dollars to convince my mother we're in love."

Chapter Six

"You'll pay me six thousand dollars to *whaaaat*?"

Wide blue eyes regarded him like he'd lost his mind, but no suspicion lurked in their depths, so Booker stayed the course. "I'll pay you to be my date for all the family events I have to attend between now and the wedding—a thousand dollars each."

Those wide eyes turned doubtful. "What are these events? I don't play polo. I never attended cotillion, and I'm not a member of the country club."

"You drink wine, right? Kate and Aaron are having a wine-tasting thing for their bachelor/bachelorette party. My parents are hosting a party. There's the rehearsal dinner, and then the wedding itself, and the reception—I count those separately."

"And I still only count five events."

"I factored in a practice date. We want this to look real."

She tipped her head to the side. "Define date, Sheriff. And while you're at it, define *real*, because I think on Craigslist people call this 'The Girlfriend Experience' and I'm pretty sure it's illegal."

"Get your mind out of the gutter, Jailbait. My proposal involves me paying you to make a series of public appearances with me, convincing my mother we have a deep emotional connection. Anything happening between us, in private, has nothing to do with this arrangement."

Strangely, drawing the fine lines between what the money covered, and what it excluded, didn't bother him. Those lines remained very clear in his mind, and even though she'd raised the question, he sensed she'd done it for the sake of argument. He wasn't making an indecent proposal, and they both knew it. Dishonest? Yes, and morally debatable, but not indecent.

Second thoughts sprouted like weeds. *You really want to do this? Lie to your family? Manipulate Lauralie into accepting your help?* He'd already conducted a ten second internal debate before he'd opened his mouth, but apparently his conscience demanded a final go/no-go check. He took stock of her, sitting beside him in a sweatshirt and cut-offs like some ghost of her teenage self, still covering any fear or uncertainty with a tough veneer of I-don't-need-anyone. She'd let down her guard with him enough to disclose the extent of her situation, and that alone felt like a breakthrough even if the confession had been an effort on her part to push him away. He'd called her on it, demonstrating he wouldn't be pushed away so easily, but she still couldn't take that extra step—accepting help. Too much pride. Too little trust. Whatever the cause, he needed to deal with it, and find a way to make it okay for her to take what he offered without sacrificing her self-respect. If the end goal required a little deceit and manipulation, so be it.

He looked at her again. She chewed on her thumbnail.

A lot of manipulation. For maximum effect, he waited another half a second before shaking his head. "Never mind. Now that I'm thinking it through, I see it's not going to work."

Her chin came up. "Why won't it work?"

Bait taken. "What I have in mind requires half a dozen convincing displays of serious, heartfelt attachment. It's too much to ask." He waited another beat before adding, "Of *you*."

She turned to face him, her arms crossed, brow ominously low. "What do you mean, 'of me'? What's wrong with *me*?"

"Nothing's wrong with you, per se, but you're thin on real-life experience. I need someone who can make this look authentic, or I'm wasting my time and money. Forget I said anything. I'll find someone else."

"Okay, first off"—she held up one finger—"I have plenty of experience. Second—"

He took hold of her wrist. "You don't do relationships. You have no experience with deep attachments."

"Oh, and you do?"

The irony of her question coaxed a laugh out of him. "You don't know everything about me, Jailbait."

That earned him a startled expression, followed immediately by a gratifying flush. *Bothers you that I've got you wondering, doesn't it?* She tried to tug her wrist free but he held on.

"Why not ask her, then?"

"Who says I haven't?"

"Wow. And she turned you down. Who found you less than irresistible?"

That she'd misinterpreted his comment was for the best. She wasn't ready. "I don't kiss and tell." He kissed the inside of her wrist and let go of her hand. She absently rubbed her thumb over the place his mouth had touched, and shot him a cautious look.

Not a single lie had passed his lips. Even so, he ought to correct her, but the flare of jealousy he'd unintentionally provoked proved a little too rewarding.

Her lips hitched into a jaded smile. "Last night suddenly makes a lot more sense."

"What are you talking about?"

"You showed up out of the blue, crashed my party, and fucked my brains out. Now I know why."

He already didn't like where this was going. "Lauralie, I don't know what you think you know, but—"

"You came looking for the time-honored cure for a bruised heart—mind-numbing rebound sex."

Okay, he *should* have corrected her. "Last night had *nothing* to do with rebound sex." And that's all he could say, because if he told her last night had been about *them*, she'd take off so fast she'd leave skid marks on the shoulder of the road.

"Don't worry." She patted his arm. "I happen to be a big proponent of mind-numbing sex. I don't need to complicate things with a bunch of pretty lies. I never have."

She didn't have the first clue what the hell she needed. "You're a cynic."

Sunlight slanted across her face, turning her eyes to sapphires. "I'm a realist. Do you honestly think most of us are cut out for forever?"

"Yeah. I do." He reached out and smoothed the little *V* from between her brows.

"Hmm. Who would have guessed you were such a rosy-eyed romantic."

"I'm not a rosy-eyed anything. I don't think it's easy. From what I can tell, it takes work, and compromise, and"—he laughed at fate's way of punishing him with this discussion— "a shitload of patience, but I know the meaning of the word commitment, and if I make a one, I stand by it. Forever."

"I know the perfect girl for you."

"You think?" He brushed her hair away from her face. Were they about to have an epiphany?

"Yep. Unfortunately she just moved to Maui."

The near-term choices were let her go or shake some sense into her. He let go. "Chelsea's a great girl, but she's not the one for me."

"Well, I'm going to give you the same advice I gave her before she left."

"What's that?"

She wrapped her arms around her body and sat with her back against the door. "Guard your heart. You let people in, and they trash it like a cheap motel room."

The strength of her belief showed in every stiff line of her body. Not for the first time, he wanted to hunt Denise Peterson down and rail at her for failing to muster up even a basic degree of accountability. Or rail at Lauralie for turning her mother's shortcomings into a personal philosophy instead of laying them precisely where they belonged—at Denise's doorstep—and expecting better of herself. But mentioning all the ways she was adopting her mother's limitations would push her away, and he wanted to reel her in. "You proved my point."

"What point?"

"You're the wrong woman for the job. You don't believe in forever, and you can't even talk about the possibility without wedging yourself into a corner and getting defensive. You think my mother won't pick up on this?" He gestured at her. "My mom misses no detail. She's not going to buy us as a couple."

Lauralie uncrossed her arms, shook them out, and then tipped her head back, to the left, and the right, working the kinks from her neck. Finally, she looked at him. "Yes, she will."

"You think you can sell her on us? How?"

"Like this." She leaned over the center console, sank her fingers into his hair, and fused her mouth to his. Her breasts landed against his chest, and even through two layers of clothes he knew she didn't have a stitch on under her sweatshirt. He imagined she was equally bare beneath the shorts.

Painful as it was to resist finding out, he fought his way back to the well of restraint he'd drunk from for too many fucking years, because he hadn't meant to turn this into a sexual challenge. Yes, he wanted her, and yes, less than twenty-four hours ago he'd unapologetically used sex to get her. Last night that move had felt fair. Today, after the universe had conspired to throw her world into a tailspin? Defining fair got much trickier.

Trickier still when she moaned and arched against him, and what started as her trying to prove something turned into her trying to ask for something.

Comfort.

Instead of good tidings, the New Year had rained a shitstorm down on her. She sought shelter. Temporary shelter, granted, but even so he wanted to be the man to give it to her. She'd accept it from him—as long as it took this form. He got a grip on her hips, hauled her onto her knees, and took control of the kiss.

Her hair swung forward, shielding them from anything beyond the kiss, but the sharp scent of smoke clung to the curls, reminding him of how easily fate could have twisted in a different direction, and he wouldn't be holding her now.

The realization set off another one of those primitive needs. This time he didn't fight it. He shoved his arm between her legs, lifted her over the console, and positioned her on her knees astride his lap. A domineering move, he acknowledged, despite the fact that it put her on top. She thought so too, judging by her reactions. She bit his lip hard enough to bruise—punishment for reminding her she wasn't in charge. At the same time, she rocked herself against his arm, still lodged at the apex of her thighs. She needed this, badly. The hot, wet seam of her shorts pressed against his skin didn't lie.

He tightened his arm, trapping her squirming hips in the angle where his flexors met his biceps.

She bucked, putting one last effort into controlling the ride, then let out a little cry and wrapped her arms around his head.

Surrender so sweet deserved a reward. He jostled her in the crook of his arm. Three times. Fast and hard. Her breasts, restrained only by her sweatshirt, bounced against his face.

"Oh. Oh. Oooooh." Her hold on him tightened. Her body trembled, then stiffened, and her husky moan filled the car.

A second later she slumped forward, face against the headrest. He turned his head and kissed the curve of her neck. "That's never going to fool my family. You'll have to try harder."

She laughed, and gave him a weak hug. "*That* will get you disowned. I meant to demonstrate how convincing I can be with a kiss, but some people" — she drew away and rolled her eyes — "don't know when to quit."

"Some people don't know better than to squirm around in my lap."

"That's a risk you run when you drag a person onto your lap." Very deliberately, she squirmed again.

He grabbed her hips to still her. "*I'm* the one who doesn't know when to quit?"

"Feels to me like we quit too soon." Despite his restraining grip, she rocked forward, managing to grind his balls and his cock in one fluid motion. While he sucked in a breath, she licked her lips seductively. "There's still plenty of work here, and I hate to leave a task unfinished."

His body ached to let her finish him, but after spending the last few hours sweating in last night's clothes, he needed a long shower before he was fit to be worked on. "Sorry, Jailbait. I instituted a firm 'No blowjobs in my parents' driveway' policy after an unfortunate incident my sophomore year of high school."

Her eyebrows lifted. "Sophomore year? My, weren't you precocious."

"I didn't say I was involved. I said it was an unfortunate incident."

"*Were* you involved?"

"I was sixteen, I'd gotten a car for my birthday, and I was in love. That's all I'll admit."

"Hey, you're the one who wants to convince your mother we're in love. Just sayin'," she added when he blocked her hand from wandering to his fly.

"I was in love with the car." He swept her hair back from her face, relieved to see the desolate look haunting her features since the fire mostly gone. He wanted to keep it that way, which meant it was time to close the deal. "But when it comes to us, I think you're right. The chemistry is very convincing."

Her expression sobered. She looked toward his parents' property and cleared her throat. "Booker, I don't pretend to be an expert on families, least of all yours, but making them think we're"—she paused and made air quotes—"'in love', might be a bad call, even if your mother is overstepping her bounds. I have nothing to lose if things go sideways, but you could damage your relationship with your parents." She turned back to him and pinned him with a serious look. "Have you thought this through?"

Her concern took him by surprise. He'd been so intent on finding an acceptable way to help her, he hadn't anticipated she'd worry about *him*. "The genius of my plan is in its simplicity. Nothing will go sideways."

She laughed and crawled off his lap. "Jesus, you're cocky."

"I'm a realist," he echoed her earlier self-assessment. "I'll pick you up tomorrow night at seven."

Confusion notched her brows. "What's tomorrow night?"

"Our first date. Wear something pretty."

• • •

Another outfit landed across the bed. Laurie sighed at the growing pile, and dug into her closet again.

The first options had seemed too dressy, and the next, way too casual. Of course, she was aiming at an unknown target, considering Booker had given her no details beyond *Wear something pretty*. She pulled a slinky blue dress out of her closet and looked at it critically before shoving it back into the closet. Too…something.

What did one wear for a fake date with the town sheriff? *Something that doesn't make you look like a hooker.*

Right. Aim for simple and classy. She pulled on the next possibility, and scolded herself for making a mountain out of such a molehill. She knew Montenido like she knew the freckles across her nose. When it came to things to do, the town didn't present endless options. Dinner. Maybe a movie. The area around the university boasted a few clubs, and during summer people liked to picnic on the beach and watch the sunset, but the only fools hanging out on the beach on a January evening were sixteen year olds looking to get laid.

So…no beach. Tempted as she was to put on cut-offs, a Montenido University tank top, and Uggs for old time's sake, she doubted Booker would laugh.

He might laugh at this, though. The generic black pencil skirt and fitted red blouse managed to scream I'm-trying-too-hard and I-have-absolutely-no-imagination at the same time. She stared at her reflection in the mirror above her dresser and added a scarf to the ensemble. Awesome. Now she looked like a flight attendant. She ripped the stupid silk square off, tossed it onto the chaise, and got to work on the blouse buttons.

She'd stressed about this date all day. Actually had to stop herself from calling him at a half dozen points during the afternoon and asking for some hint of what he had in mind for tonight. Pathetic.

Worse, she knew the indecisiveness stemmed from nerves. Booker trusted her with his problem, and asked for her help solving it. She needed to get her side of things right. Unfortunately, New Year's Eve had shown that when left to her own devices, she looked like she shopped at Denise's R Us. In an effort to muster up some classy, she ended up overthinking things and driving herself crazy.

He's picking you up. If you're dressed wrong, he'll say something, and you'll change.

Dressed *wrong*? She stepped out of her black peep-toe heels. Where had that come from?

Her temper started to simmer—mostly at herself, but also at him, for asking her out in the first place and turning her into a self-conscious freak.

Enough. How about you wear what you want, and if he doesn't like it, he can change his plans for the evening?

She looked at herself in the mirror, wearing nothing except her lucky black bra and matching panties. The sexy curves of her white chaise beckoned from behind her. A sudden, vivid fantasy played out in the mirror. Booker sat on the chaise, with her astride him. One tug from him was all it would take to rend the thin straps of her bra. Then he tangled his long fingers in the back of her thong and slowly pull it off… Heat licked her skin, even as anticipation tightened it.

Hell, she should just meet him at the door like this. What was the point of the date anyway? Some kind of test? A dress rehearsal to make sure she cleaned up all right before he paraded her in front of his family? Because if it was, *screw* him and his six thousand bucks. He could find someone else— some debutant with the right upbringing who instinctively chose the perfect I-don't-know-what-the-fuck-we're-doing-tonight outfit.

The doorbell chimed, interrupting her internal rant, and before she could talk herself out of it, she stormed to the door all horny and pissed, flung it open, and pulled him inside by his belt buckle. As soon as he cleared the threshold she slammed the door behind him, pivoted on her heel, and stalked down the hall toward her bedroom. "I decided we're staying in tonight."

His footsteps assured her he followed, but when she turned to face him, he didn't stop coming at her. Instead, he backed her up, spun her around, and bent her over the high arm of the chaise. Next thing she knew, his big palm cracked across her ass, and a current of perverse pleasure ricocheted through her.

His voice rolled over her gasp. "Did you even look through the peephole? What if it hadn't been me?" He brought his hand down again, but lower this time, hitting places between her thighs and making them sing.

"Who says I thought it was you?"

He bent her into a deeper angle, kicked her feet apart, and delivered an all-too-fleeting blow right over ground zero. The impact stung sensitive nerve endings and forced another gasp out of her.

"You're spoiling for a fight, aren't you? Tell you what, Lauralie, I'm going to adjust your mood, and then you're going to get dressed, and we're going out."

"Don't bet on it, Booker."

"We're betting on it." He traced the line of her thong and she pushed her face into the cushion to keep from begging. When he grazed her clit with his knuckle she struggled not to chase his touch. "I'll bet I can make you come in the next ten seconds. If I lose, send me home. If I win, we go to dinner, and you sit across from me in your drenched panties, remembering exactly who got you there."

She wanted to warn him a smart man would run for the door, because when it came to her, even if he won, he lost, but what came out of her mouth was, "I hope you didn't make reservations."

Something landed on the cushion beside her head. His phone. She glimpsed ten seconds on the timer, but then he stroked her again, moving that diabolical knuckle in a circle, and her vision blurred. Trembles started in her knees and quickly migrated to her thighs. Everything ached. Everything throbbed. She held her breath and willed herself to endure. Do them both a favor and end this farce before one of them did something that couldn't be undone. Ten seconds? Surely she could hold out for ten seconds.

He caught her clit between his fingers and squeezed. Pressure built in her lungs. Places deep inside her wound so tight tears stung her eyes. Every nerve in her body felt as if it originated at the stunningly sensitive knot of flesh trapped in his clasp.

He bent over her so his words flowed directly into her ear. "Tell me, Jailbait, how close are you?" She might have had it in her to tell him, "Close only counts in horseshoes," but he didn't wait for a reply. Instead he gave the tip of her clit a ruthless flick and sent her over, releasing a spasm of pleasure strong enough to curl her spine. Her breath escaped from her lungs on a moan of relief.

A second spasm waited behind the first. Seeing as how her noble intentions had failed, she rocked her hips and prepared for more, but the hand between her legs abruptly withdrew, and what promised to be an exquisitely intense aftershock immediately faded. Desperate to recapture the subsiding sensation, she clenched her thighs and tried to close her legs. His foot between hers thwarted her, and the maddening ghost of an orgasm floated off.

His lips brushed the rim of her ear. "I win." He angled his phone so she could see the screen and watch the last two seconds tick by.

"That doesn't count, and you know it." Damn it, she sounded whiny instead of rightfully pissed.

"Why? Because I didn't service you to your heart's content?" His hand took the back route between her legs again, fingertips leading. She widened her stance and lifted onto her tiptoes to give him a proper opportunity to make it up to her.

Apparently he had different ideas. He swirled his fingers over the silk stretched across her sex, and then drew a lazy design on her bare skin with his fingertip. "That wasn't our bet, was it?"

Damn him. "No."

"What was our bet?"

"Ten seconds to make me come."

"And did you? Speak up, Jailbait. Yes or no?"

He knew very well she had. He was painting her ass with the evidence. "Yes, but — "

"No buts." He slapped hers, hard enough to suggest she hadn't cornered the market on frustration, and stepped away. "I won. Get dressed."

Chapter Seven

Booker walked out of her bedroom, parked himself by her front window, and dragged a hand through his hair hard enough to make his scalp sting. The pain didn't much distract from the real agony centered much lower, but it was the best he could manage at the moment, short of banging his head against a wall. If his hard-on didn't subside soon he might break down and try blunt head trauma.

A cautious breath brought some oxygen to his deprived brain, and a small measure of equilibrium followed. Enough to silently acknowledge the initial five minutes of his first date with Lauralie Peterson qualified as an exercise in self-torture. He should have expected as much. She came with lots of warning labels, most of which she'd proudly applied herself. He'd never mistaken her for a gentle soul.

While he appreciated her complexities, tonight's behavior wasn't especially difficult to interpret. She'd attempted to hijack control of the evening. Why remained a mystery, but she hadn't opened her door wearing nothing but underwear to initiate a conversation about tonight's plans — a conversation he would have been perfectly happy to have, for the record—she'd done it to initiate a power struggle. Something had set her off, and instead of discussing it with him she'd resorted to the tactics experience had taught her were most likely to result in her getting her way.

No matter how much it killed him to resist, he had to. If he gave in to the tactic, even over something as inconsequential in the grand scheme of things as whether they went out for dinner tonight, he was just like any other guy she'd known. Fools who settled for her body instead of trying to figure out what was going on in her mind. She'd lose respect for him—as well she should—and he'd lose respect for himself. They both deserved better.

The knowledge helped keep his less reasoned instincts in check—the ones picturing her bent over the demure white sofa with her hips lifted high and his cock buried in the welcoming heat between her thighs.

The *ding* of his phone signaling an incoming text also helped get those rampant instincts under control, especially when he pulled it out and saw Aaron's name on the screen.

Favor. Call Katie and tell her you need my help tonight. Dinner's on me.

Why do I need your help?

The reason doesn't matter. Make some shit up...you need my help buying shoes for the wedding.

Shoe shopping? WTF? Should we get pedicures first?

Bloody buggering hell, just give her a reason, or I'm stuck having dinner with the ice queen.

Was that some sort of British slang? Dinner with the ice queen?

I'm busy.

Stop wanking.

That bit of slang he recognized.

Fuck off, pervert. I'm taking Lauralie to dinner.

Ah. So you're wanking off later.

The insulting prediction made him smile.

Exactly.

Going to the pub near her place?

He knew where this was heading.

Don't even think about it. Come anywhere near Delaney's, I'll have you arrested and deported.

Untwist your knickers. I won't be there.

Before Booker could type in an appropriate threat in response, Aaron signed off with a fist, followed by an eggplant.

Bastard. But a smile tugged at the corners of his mouth. Receiving obscene, go-fuck-yourself emoticons from his sister's fiancé restored his faith in human nature. He touched the button to bring up his home screen and slid the phone into the pocket of his jeans, feeling calmer than he had since arriving on Lauralie's doorstep.

His blood pressure spiked again a second later when she emerged from her bedroom immersed in a slouchy gray sweater, black leggings, and tall, black boots. She'd scooped her hair into a sexy knot at the back of her head, but some stray curls escaped to tease her neck…and his cock.

Halfway down the hall she paused and leaned over to give one boot a tug. The wide neckline of her sweater gaped.

Choose another view or you're never going to make it to dinner.

He shifted his attention to a silver chain bracelet encircling her wrist. Charms dangled from it, bouncing off each other every time she moved. He imagined them jangling rhythmically while she clung to that big iron bed of hers and he drove into her.

Good job. That's much better.

When she straightened, her eyes found his. "Problem?"

"None." The vicious pounding in his dick made his response harsher than he intended.

Her eyes flashed. She crossed her arms and firmed her chin. "Good, because I'm fresh out of Armani. I don't know what you were expecting, but this is what you get. If you don't like it, we can end this date right now."

What the fuck Armani had to do with anything, he couldn't say, but the mystery of what had set her off immediately resolved. She'd worked herself into a mood over what to wear. He'd work on getting to the underlying reason after he reassured her. A couple steps closed the distance between them. When they stood toe-to-toe, he gave her a slow once-over. "You look beautiful. Is that what you need to hear?"

Even as pink crept into her cheeks, she rolled her eyes, muttered, "Men," and swept past him. "You wouldn't understand."

The exasperation in her voice pulled a laugh out of him. "Two nights ago you told me you always dress to please yourself. Why would I expect you to do otherwise tonight?"

She stalked to the entryway closet and yanked it open. "I don't know, Booker." Hangers scraped as she searched through the garments. "You're the one who wants this…trial run, or whatever you call it."

And there it was. He wanted to kick himself for leaving her with the impression tonight amounted to some sort of audition she might pass or fail. He walked over, silently hemming her in between the closet and his body. She pulled a short, black leather jacket off a hanger, and then turned and glared at him. He held his ground.

"I call it a date. You seem unfamiliar with the concept. See, what happens is two people go out for a meal, some conversation, and a chance to enjoy each other's company."

"We could enjoy each other's company right here, but apparently that doesn't interest you—"

He cupped a hand to the back of her head to protect her skull, and pressed her against the doorframe, pinning her hips with his. "Does it feel like I'm not interested?"

Her breath steamed his jaw. "Then *why* are we going out?"

"It's what people in a relationship do."

"We're not in a relationship—"

"We are for the next six weeks." And he didn't intend to waste a single one of them. "Don't look so annoyed, Jailbait. You might actually end up having a good time."

Blond brows arched. "In my experience the more time we spend together fully clothed, the more likely we'll end up bored out of our minds."

He took the jacket from her, gestured for her to turn around, and helped her into it. With his mouth close to her ear, he said, "The woman wearing wet panties is worried about being bored?"

"Sorry to tell you this, Booker, but my panties aren't wet."

"They will be, before dinner is over."

She turned and patted his cheek. "Not going to happen."

He caught her hand, brought it to his mouth, and sank his teeth into the pad of flesh below her thumb, biting just hard enough to make her eyes darken. "What makes you so sure?"

"I'm not wearing any panties."

. . .

Laurie smoothed Scarlet Seduction over her upper lip, then the lower. Once both were coated, she pressed them together and let them part with a little pop. With the small chore attended to, she officially ran out of reasons to loiter in the ladies' room at Delaney's. Booker was in the bar, somewhere, ordering drinks while they waited for a table to open. In truth, she didn't even need to use the restroom. She excused herself because she needed a moment to recover after their walk from her apartment to the restaurant.

Walking a quarter of a mile along well-maintained sidewalks didn't elevate her pulse in the least, but walking a quarter of a mile with Booker's fingers casually threaded through hers and his thumb caressing her palm with steady strokes that enflamed every one of her overheated nerve endings? That quickened her pulse. And she had a sneaking suspicion he knew it.

Stupid, letting such a simple gesture throw her off her game, but her system simply hadn't known how to react when he'd reached down and taken her hand. She wasn't a hold hands kind of girl. Best she could recall she'd never walked hand in hand with anyone. Maybe Chelsea, when they were little, but otherwise? Nope. If she decided to let a man touch her, they didn't waste time holding her hand. What was the point?

Except maybe there was one because five minutes of strolling hand in hand with Booker sent her straight to the restroom to wrestle with her equilibrium. What was wrong with her?

I don't know, but the next time you go on a date with Booker, wear underwear.

Excellent plan. She pushed through the restroom door. The hum of conversations immediately surrounded her. It took some doing to maneuver her way through the crowd to where Booker stood beside the only empty barstool. He chatted with the bartender—a tall, sun-bleached stud named Jessie, who was basically a golden retriever trapped in the body of a man. Jessie's easy-going smile dimmed when he looked her way.

"Hey, Laurie. 'Sup?"

He extended an arm across the bar for a hug. She leaned in and gave him one, a little surprised when he didn't let go right away. A quick glance at Booker revealed nothing. "What's up with you, Jessie?"

"I heard about the fire. I'm super-bummed for you. And for me." He slowly uncurled his arm, and gave her the puppy dog eyes. "I loved your maple-glazed waffle donuts."

The weight of the loss settled on her again. In her preoccupation with Booker and this date, she'd momentarily forgotten the reason she'd agreed to this charade in the first place. "Hopefully I'll be able to rebuild soon." *Assuming you repay the deposits, and your loan, and don't go bankrupt in the meantime.*

His smile returned. "Awesome. Let me know how I can help."

She picked up the glass of white wine sitting on the bar next to Booker's beer. "This helps."

"Dude, wait. That drink is not for you. It's for Booker's date. She's in the restroom."

She glanced at Booker, who appeared to be stifling a laugh. "I'm back from the restroom." So saying, she took a purposeful drink.

Granted, Jessie read the subtleties of a wave better than he read the subtleties of a situation, but it took what Laurie considered an insultingly long time before he slapped one hand to his forehead and lifted the other to Booker for a welcome-to-the-club fist bump. Also wrong. Booker was smart enough to dig for his wallet right then and "miss" the not-so-secret handshake.

"Oh, wow. You're his date. I did *not* see that coming. But"—he regarded them for a moment, and nodded as if happy with what he saw—"cool."

Not really, but they'd managed to convince one person they were on a legit date. She called that a win, and toasted herself with another swallow.

When Jessie stepped down the bar to serve other customers, she turned to find Booker's eyes on her. Knowing and persistent. Like he awaited a confession.

Why was he giving her that look? She checked her earrings to make sure she hadn't accidentally worn a mismatched pair. Nope. The oversize silver hoops matched. "What?"

A dark eyebrow arched.

Oh. "Once. A while ago. Don't you dare throw stones." She shrugged out of her jacket and draped it over the back of the barstool. "You're no virgin. I can name names."

His laugh startled her. "I have no intention of getting into a stone throwing contest with you. And for the record, I don't give a single fuck who you entertained yourself with before New Year's Eve." He caught her chin and pulled her close for a hard kiss that ended way too soon. When he eased away his smile returned—the confident smile. "You're mine now."

Mine. She understood the context of his comment, but even so, the word uncaged wings in her stomach. Another big swallow of wine settled the annoying flutters. "I'm yours *for* now, pursuant to our…arrangement, which, judging by Jessie's reaction, is going to be a hard sell."

He rested a forearm arm on the bar, and leaned toward her. "What makes you say that? We sold Jessie."

"Please. You can't judge by what came out of his mouth. Reactions speak louder than words. Even with me standing right beside you, it took him a full minute to realize I was your date. The sheriff and the troublemaker don't make the most intuitive of matches." Nor did a guy from a wealthy, respectable family and a girl whose family tree might as well be a cactus. The list of reasons they made a laughable couple went on and on…

"You're not a troublemaker."

"Interesting statement, coming from you. I'm pretty sure I didn't give myself a nickname like Jailbait." Shit. This topic led down memory lane. A journey she didn't want to make. Seeking escape, she reached for her wineglass.

His hand covered her wrist, stalling her. She looked up to find him staring at her with a serious expression. "I called you Jailbait because I wanted to get your attention, and make you understand the risks inherent in your situation. Lecturing you would have wasted my breath and your time."

"Hey." She shrugged, and slid her wrist out from under his hand. "The shoe fit." Hoping that put an end to the conversation, she lifted the glass to her lips.

"You couldn't see yourself the way I saw you, back then." He rested his arm on the bar and regarded her, but she had a funny feeling he was looking back in time.

"You saw a troublemaker."

"I saw a trouble-*magnet*. A beautiful girl who looked more mature than she was. Vulnerable in ways you didn't appreciate." His laugh sounded slightly pained. "You fucking terrified me."

"*I* terrified *you*? Why?"

"I was afraid I wouldn't be able to protect you."

Oh, God. This man. A part of her wanted to wrap her arms around those save-the-world shoulders of his and hug him for giving a shit about a smart-mouthed brat who couldn't even inspire an ounce of concern from her own mother. Instead, she put her glass down and pushed at the sleeve of her sweater. "I didn't need protecting."

"You did, first and foremost from yourself. Sometimes you still do." He trailed his fingers over her jaw.

It occurred to her Booker touched her whenever and however he pleased. Not just sexually, though there was always a spark whenever their skin brushed, but more like she…belonged.

You belong to yourself. You look after yourself.

She straightened and shook her head. Shook off the gentle caress. "I haven't been jailbait for years, and I outgrew any need for protection a long time ago."

"One of the first things you learn in law enforcement is we all need someone watching our backs. It doesn't make you weak. It makes you human."

The warning sirens sounded again, but not as loud, or maybe she was just getting better at ignoring them because she wanted to hear what he had to say. "You had my back?"

"Always." A smile raised the corner of his mouth. "I'll always have your back. But you're right about the other thing."

"What other thing?"

"You're not a kid anymore. You grew up, and into a smart, hardworking, accomplished woman. I'm proud of you."

Warmth crept up her neck and into her face. Jesus, was she actually blushing for the second time in one night? Before she could point out her accomplishments had burned to the ground yesterday, the hostess appeared and invited them to follow her. Booker motioned her ahead of him, and soon they were seated next to each other at a small corner table.

The hostess handed them menus, and then leveled an inquiring gaze on Laurie. "Another wine?"

She froze in the process of raising her glass to her lips and realized she only had a swallow left. Pounding wine smacked of a Denise coping mechanism, so she put her glass down and pushed it away. "I'm good."

The girl assured them their server would be over shortly and retreated. Booker shifted in his chair. A hard thigh brushed hers. "Are you good, Lauralie?"

His voice held no hint of challenge. He really wanted to know how she was doing. More alarming, she was pathetically tempted to tell him. Rest her head on his strong shoulder and pour out her troubles. "Just dandy." She crossed her legs and pulled herself together. "Okay, we're on a date. What now?"

He lifted her fist from where it rested on the table, and cradled it in his palm. Her hand—her average, unremarkable hand—looked small and delicate compared to his, especially when he ran this thumb over her knuckles. "Now we engage in the lost art of conversation."

"What do you want to talk about?"

"Whatever's on your mind. Have you notified your insurance company yet?"

Speaking of troubles. She plucked at a loose thread on the tablecloth. "Let's not ruin a perfectly good fake date with reality."

"I'll take that as a yes." His thumb made the trip over her knuckles again.

She sighed and nodded. "Yes. I actually met with my agent yesterday afternoon at the bakery."

"That was fast."

"The benefit of going with a local agent. He's not like a good neighbor, he *is* a good neighbor, and if I need to file a claim on New Year's Day, he's there. Anyway, he walked me through my coverage, took photos, and helped me complete and submit the initial claim paperwork."

"Did he mention next steps and give you any timeframe?"

Another sigh threatened, but she swallowed it. "He said pretty much what Chief Nelson said. The company will do its own investigation, I'm obligated to cooperate, and these things take time."

His hand settled on her knee, big and comforting. "Nelson read it as an electrical fire, which is pretty damn straightforward. As far as the claim itself, I'm guessing there are no curve balls. You weren't stockpiling mink coats or laptops with your sugar and spice?"

"I was fresh out of mink coats. My losses are total, but not out of the ordinary for my business."

"Okay then, it might take their lab a few weeks to corroborate Nelson's opinion on cause, and their adjudicator will need to spend some time with your claim, but there's not a lot for the investigator to chew on. You've given them a clean set of facts."

"Yeah…" Except there was one not-so-clean fact lurking in the shadows.

She dredged up what felt like a half-hearted smile. Everybody knew Babycakes had been closed New Year's Day, and she'd confirmed to Booker, Nelson, and her insurance agent that she'd personally locked up the prior afternoon. But nobody had asked if she'd returned to the premises any time after closing. She hadn't volunteered the information because…well…she wasn't stupid. It looked bad. Discovering she'd not only been in the bakery the morning of the fire, but had cleaned out her safe, would definitely give the investigator something to chew on. Something that maybe looked and tasted a lot like insurance fraud. It might take years to rebuild Babycakes. If she got the chance at all.

She also had to think of Booker's reputation. If the investigation turned up anything off-putting and they pointed the finger at her, there'd be no stopping people from jumping to the wrong conclusion.

Would they fire Booker for dating a suspected arsonist?

No. Nelson already had a decent idea of when and how the blaze had started, and she hadn't seen anything to confirm or dispute his impressions during her short stop to get Denise her go-the-fuck-away money. Bringing her mother into it, airing that nasty bit of dirty laundry, added nothing useful to the investigation. Things would fall into place. They *had* to.

"Meanwhile"—he squeezed her knee—"you've got time to evaluate what worked well the first time around, and what you want to do differently."

"You sound just like Chelsea."

"I doubt that. Her voice is much higher than mine."

"Har. You know what I meant. By the time she finished giving me a long-distance pep talk yesterday evening, she almost had me believing this was all a blessing in disguise. Babycakes will be back, bigger and better than ever, and to help make it happen, she's determined to stake this big bonus she might get at her new job."

His brows lowered a notch. "Let me get this straight. Accepting a loan from me violates your standards of self-sufficiency, but it's perfectly fine to take Chelsea's money?"

Okay, somehow she'd offended him, but dammit, there was a difference. She pushed up her sleeves and propped her elbows on the table. "I didn't take anything. There's nothing to take. Her bonus is completely speculative at this point."

"But if she gets it?"

Of course he wasn't going to let her punt the question. Fine. She leaned back in her chair and crossed her arms. "Then yes, if my best friend wants to invest her hard-earned money in Babycakes—"

"You, Lauralie, are a snob."

"Are you kidding me? I'm not the one who grew up at the top of the hill, with my wealthy family and my fat trust fund."

He leaned forward, into her space, and she belatedly realized she'd made a tactical error. She'd literally given up ground.

"No, that would be me. I've got money to spare, but it's not hard-earned enough for you."

The softly delivered accusation nevertheless packed the power to momentarily stun her, and make her question her motives. Did she disqualify people from certain roles in her life simply because they'd been born with advantages? And if so, did that make her some kind of reverse snob, or did it make her smart enough to know taking money from a rich guy—particularly a rich guy she was sleeping with—made her look like a gold-digging whore, and people around here already expected that kind of behavior from Denise Peterson's daughter?

"I'm not a snob. And, as it happens, I am accepting money from you." She glanced around, and then leaned in, too, attempting to reclaim the territory she'd ceded. "In fact, I'm on the clock right now."

He didn't give an inch. "That's different, and you know it."

It was different, but the six grand he'd pay her for helping him keep his mother out of his personal life for the next little while was as far down the path as she intended to go. They both had good reason to keep their business discreet, and, frankly, nobody would question where she got the money to refund a handful of deposits. The stickier question would be why wasn't it sitting in her safe in the first place. But people sure as hell would question where she came up with the kind of funds needed to reopen the bakery, and if the answer was Ethan Booker, she'd find herself on the receiving end of a whole lot of unflattering assumptions. So would he, for that matter, but the nice thing about sitting at the top of the social hill meant, generally, shit rolled down.

"Look, I am *not* a snob—"

"Oh my God, Booker!" A female voice broke in. "This place is crazy tonight. Can we join you?"

Chapter Eight

Booker turned and aimed a stare at his sister intended to convey one word. *No*. A quick glance at the scalpel-thin woman standing beside Kate, clutching a Hermes bag, and looking like she might contract a disease if she inhaled too deeply had him upping the silent message to a *Hell, no!*

Not that it would do any good. Kate hadn't forgiven him for the New Year's Day hangover. Her guileless smile tightened at one corner, just enough to issue a silent message of her own. *Revenge is mine.*

Not if he had anything to say about it. But he didn't, as it turned out, because Lauralie gestured to the empty chairs and said, "Of course we don't mind. Have a seat."

Goddammit. Downtown Montenido boasted at least a hundred dining options, and Delaney's had never been at the top of Kate's list. Bad luck couldn't be blamed for bringing his sister and her notoriously uptight wedding planner — Miranda McQueen — to his table tonight. Aaron's cryptic comment about dinner with the ice queen floated through his mind. Yeah, he'd been sacrificed like a lamb.

Manners dictated he seat the ladies and make introductions, so he rose and pulled out a chair for Miranda, and then Kate. As he dropped a kiss on her cheek, he muttered, "I hope Aaron's having a nice evening."

"Shame about his last-minute plans. He'll be sorry he missed you."

"Oh, he'll be sorry." Fucker. He rested a hand on Lauralie's shoulder. "Meet my sister, Kate, and our family friend, Miranda."

"The pleasure's all ours," Kate beamed. "You look—" She paused as a busboy swooped in with two additional place settings and waters. When he retreated, she continued, "You look so familiar to me. Are you local?"

"Native," Lauralie confirmed, and took a sip of water.

"Really?" Miranda chimed in, frowning slightly. He could practically hear her flipping through the pages of the social register stored in her frontal lobe. The woman could trace her bloodline to Montenido's founding fathers, and she'd married into equally vested families—twice. She was incredibly well connected, and she prided herself on knowing who was who. "What's your last name?"

"Peterson," Lauralie answered.

"Peterson…Peterson…any relation to Stu and Bitsy Peterson? I did their daughter's wedding last summer. Pink fantasy, like a fairy tale. We transformed a team of white horses into pink unicorns to lead the carriage that whisked them away on their honeymoon—*Montenido Magazine* featured a picture on their cover."

"Sounds…spectacular," Lauralie responded, "but no, I'm not related to Stu and Bitsy."

"Oh. Hmm." Miranda's Botox-impaired frown returned. "I thought I knew all the Petersons in Montenido."

Kate glanced at the ceiling, and shook her head. "Only the ones paying for big, splashy weddings."

Miranda preened a little at the comment, and then inspected the rim of her glass, before taking a careful sip.

Kate turned her attention to Lauralie. "How did you and Booker meet?"

Lauralie swirled the last of her wine around her glass, then swallowed and cocked a brow at him. "He busted me."

Miranda made a choking sound before erupting into a series of hacking coughs. Kate leaned across the table, all smiles and curiosity. "What for?"

"I didn't bust you," Booker interjected, before things went completely off the rails. "It was ten years ago, and she was out after curfew. I gave her a warning and a ride home."

"Wow." Kate propped her chin in her hand. "You got mercy out of my hard-ass brother. That's impressive. What do you do nowadays?"

Lauralie's small grin told him she enjoyed hearing his sister classify him as a hard-ass. "I own…" Her grin faded. "Scratch that, I *owned* Babycakes Bakery."

Kate scooted closer to the table, oblivious to the implications of Lauralie's use of the past tense. "My assistant raves about your place." She tapped Miranda. "You know Babycakes. The cute little shop in Nido Plaza with the…"

"With the logo inspired by a mud flap." Miranda's gaze cut to Lauralie. "Yes. Now I know *exactly* who you are."

The hint of extra frost in her voice wasn't lost on Booker. Old rumors swirled in his memory like snow flurries—annoying and insubstantial debris about Miranda's second divorce involving infidelity on her husband's part. He had a sinking feeling Denise's name might have been in the mix, but Lauralie's impassive expression suggested she neither knew, nor particularly cared, about old rumors.

Apparently Miranda preferred to focus on current events as well, because she went on. "I understand your cute little shop met with misfortune yesterday."

Kate looked from Miranda to Lauralie. "What happened?" But then her eyes clouded as awareness dawned. "Oh, no. The fire at Nido Plaza. I heard about it, but I didn't realize... My God, I am so sorry."

He took Lauralie's hand, and laced her cold fingers through his.

She thanked Kate, and gave his hand the smallest of squeezes, before doing the thing guaranteed to divert attention from her. She asked about the wedding. Within moments, Miranda McQueen was holding court, passing judgment on themes, color schemes, and other matters destined to suck away every ounce of his testosterone. He concentrated on all the ways he'd kick Aaron's ass next time he saw his future brother-in-law.

A waiter approached. Booker recognized him as a local, but couldn't put a name to the face. Based on age, he figured Lauralie probably knew him. The way the man's blue eyes scanned the table and stalled on her confirmed his guess. Booker got the distinct impression the rest of the room had just disappeared for blue eyes. He blushed to the roots of his dark hair, and mumbled, "Hi, Laurie."

Aw, hell. Another one. He draped his arm along the back of her chair.

She looked up, and immediately smiled. "Hey, Scott. Great to see you."

"Great to see you, too. You look...great."

Great. Testosterone levels restored, Booker skimmed his fingers along the curve of her neck. Too bad their waiter's attention never wavered from her face.

"You, too," she replied. "Are you home on break?" To the table, she added, "Scott's in his—sorry, I forget—third or fourth year of medical school?"

"Third year. We're on break now, so I'm helping my folks out while I'm home. I fly back tomorrow night."

The information led Booker to a positive ID. Scott Delaney. His parents owned the restaurant.

"I know it's last minute, but maybe we could…um…get together later, and catch up?" The blush returned.

Booker trailed his fingers over her earlobe and toyed with her earring. The flash caught lover boy's eye, and the hopeful smile disappeared.

Sorry, Scottie.

Lauralie shot him an *I've-got-this* look before turning her attention to her admirer. "I'm sorry. I've got plans for later."

"Oh, hey, no problem." Scott cleared his throat and pressed on. "Maybe next time?"

Maybe never. Lauralie's hand rested on the table. He slid his palm under hers, threaded their fingers, and deliberately moved their linked hands to his leg—and had the satisfaction of hearing her noncommittal reply hitch in her throat. He kept her hand while Scott took their orders, but when the waiter departed and the conversation turned again to Kate's nuptials, he shifted in his chair and, beneath the screen of the tablecloth, moved their hands to her lap.

She spared him a raised eyebrow, but otherwise continued with the riveting discussion of veil lengths. He released her hand and eased his fingers between her crossed thighs. Lean muscles jumped under his palm, and then she uncrossed her legs. Despite the invitation, he didn't explore. He simply kept his hand on her thigh, heavy and still.

A corresponding heaviness flowed into his cock. Persistent, but on the right side of the pain/pleasure spectrum. Lauralie replied to something Kate said, and ran restless fingers along the wide, slouchy neckline of her sweater. The gray knit slipped down to reveal a slender shoulder and the narrow strap of her bra.

The heaviness advanced to an ache. She fiddled with her sweater again, and squirmed in her chair. He tightened his grip on her leg. Without looking his way, she slipped her hand under the table and purposefully grazed his cock before settling on his thigh.

He coughed into his fist to cover a groan, and watched the corner of her mouth twist into a devious smirk. He retaliated by stroking a finger along the inseam of her leggings while Miranda and Kate debated the appropriateness of children at weddings. Miranda referred to them as pint-sized party crashers.

Her hand trembled as she reached for her water. She emptied the glass in a single gulp.

"Would you like more?" he murmured, and inched his finger higher.

"I—"

"Speaking of party crashers," Miranda interjected, "how long is your mother in town?"

Lauralie jerked back as if someone had slapped her. The pretty flush faded from her cheeks, and she shifted out of his grasp. "My mother isn't in town."

"She most certainly is. I saw her New Year's Eve. She made an appearance at the Montenido Arts Council party I planned at Las Ventanas. I walked her out personally, with the aid of security."

Sadly, that sounded exactly like Denise. His direct experience with the woman was limited, though uniformly negative. She'd been part of a group arrest for public drunkenness he and Halloran had made one Fourth of July when he'd been a rookie. Another deputy and he had picked her up for shoplifting from a liquor store a few years later. He had secondhand knowledge of some additional incidents, but he wasn't aware of her visiting Montenido since she'd moved to Los Angeles. He definitely hadn't known she'd turned up recently. A glance to his right, however, told him the same couldn't be said for his date. The slight relaxing of her shoulders gave her up.

"She left New Year's Day," Lauralie replied. "I drove her to the train station."

"When?" His question came out sharp, but, dammit, this was new information. Why hadn't she said something to him?

Her eyes flicked to his, then away. She ran the tip of her tongue over her upper lip. "It doesn't matter. She's gone."

Counterarguments leaped to his lips, but Scott arrived, balancing plates like a guy who'd grown up waiting tables, and reminding him they were in the middle of dinner with Kate and Miranda. He'd ask later. He knew how to bide his time.

He also knew when someone was hiding something.

• • •

Mist-heavy air cooled Laurie's skin. She tightened her hold on the jacket she carried because she was too warm to wear it, and tried to blame Booker for her overheated condition. Resting his arm around the back of her chair, touching her leg, casually handling her at every opportunity. Even if most of the contact was for show, a girl could only withstand so much. The show appeared to have adequately offended Miranda McQueen's strict social sensibilities, and completely convinced his sister they were dating, not to mention Scott and Jessie. Hell, if she didn't know better…

But she did. She drew in a breath and let it out slowly. At the beginning of the evening it had been easy to forget reality, but after Miranda had looked at her like a sleazy social climber, and then mentioned seeing her mother on New Year's Eve, she'd felt the difference in his touch. At first, he'd been playing with her, almost competitively upping the stakes in a game aimed at slowly and deliberately driving her out of her mind. Afterward, the playfulness disappeared from his touch. The sweep of his fingers on her shoulder, or his hand resting on her arm still advanced the charade, but—maybe this was her guilty conscience messing with her—she sensed an undercurrent of something else.

It was still there, in the clasp of his hand, something inescapable and authoritative. And *that's* what had her sweating right now. Booker wanted details about her mom's visit.

The thought of admitting Denise had shown up to extort money from her was humiliating enough, but admitting she'd given in to the demand? She'd sooner choke on her own tongue. Plus telling Booker the entire truth inevitably opened a huge can of worms. He'd insist she tell her insurance company, for starters, and that put too much at risk. Her mother had a reputation, and people around here assumed she was cut from the same cheap cloth. Nelson might think all signs pointed to an electrical fire, but what if they didn't? What if there was just enough doubt for the insurance adjusters to point the finger at her, the woman who cleaned out her safe hours before the shop burned to the ground?

She'd lose everything.

Worst of all, Booker would be disappointed in her. She didn't think she could take that. Tonight he'd told her he was proud of her, and though she hadn't expected the words, they mattered to her. He trusted her, too, and that also mattered. Coming clean meant losing both. On the other hand, if she let him ask questions, not coming clean meant telling a bald-faced lie—something she'd managed to avoid doing so far, though some might argue deliberate omission amounted to the same thing.

Distraction seemed like her best option, and she knew exactly what men found most distracting about her. As they neared her front door, she turned to him, letting her breast brush his arm, and her mouth hover close to his ear. "Are you coming in, or are you going to make a liar out of me?" *Or both.*

He stopped on her doorstep, and looked down at her. Streetlights cast a glow, but his eyes remained shadowed and inscrutable. "How would I do that?"

She swept her hand under his sweater and along the rugged terrain of his abs. "I told Scott I had plans for tonight."

His hand found hers through his sweater, and covered it. Didn't encourage her, or brush her away, just held her there. After a moment the corner of his mouth lifted. "You did."

The small grin loosened the stiffness in her shoulders. Situation defused. Everything was going to be all right. She slid her hand down the flat plane of his stomach, until her fingers hooked into the waist of his pants. "He was a little slower on the uptake than Jessie." She resisted mentioning Miranda had sized up the situation immediately, and was probably on the phone with Booker's mother right now, warning the woman a tacky baker from the wrong side of town had ambitions involving her only son. Meanwhile, Booker had the nerve to call *her* a snob.

His teeth flashed in the moonlight. "Scott was too busy making his move on the one that got away to accurately assess the situation."

The comment paused her in the process of closing the space between them, even though her nipples were already tight and tingly in anticipation. A laugh escaped before she could tamp down on the cynical sound. "The one that got away? I thought you didn't want to venture into this minefield?"

"This is not a minefield." He lifted her jacket from her arm and hung it on the doorknob, and then he splayed a hand at the center of her back and pressed their bodies together. His big thigh eased between hers. "It's a fact."

Pressure built everywhere they touched, along with an urgent need for friction. She couldn't keep still, so she rose up on her toes and rubbed against him. "I hate to break it to you, but I wasn't the one that got away. Actually, I always suspected I was his first."

"You were undoubtedly his first." His hand journeyed to her ass, and hauled her closer, so her toes barely touched the ground. She had no choice but to lean on him. Let him keep them upright with his strength. His mouth cruised along the side of her neck. "He looks at you with the awestruck wonder a guy reserves for the girl who shows him his first glimpse of heaven. You're the one who got away because he never got another shot with you. Nobody has. Except me."

The truth of his observation shook her almost as much as the certainty in his voice. Yet another reason why conversation with Booker was a dangerous thing. Fear that she actually had no secrets from the man kept her quiet, but when she didn't immediately answer, he scraped his teeth along the curve of her shoulder, and challenged, "Fact?"

Honesty shivered out of her. "Y-yes."

He muttered something, which sounded like, "He'll never get another shot at you," but she couldn't be sure. She could barely concentrate on his words. The hard, thick length of his cock nestled against her stomach like a promise.

"Since we're doing so well with facts, share one more with me." His thumb strummed along her spine. He drew back and looked at her. "Did your mother's visit have anything to do with why I woke up alone on New Year's Day?"

Her heartbeat quickened. The question dispelled any notion her effort at distraction worked. None of her tricks worked on him. She had no control over Booker.

Control? What a joke. Practically every aspect of her life eluded her control. Her mother, who continued to find ways to bleed her, and probably would until she sucked her dry. Her burned up dream, which might never rise from the ashes if she answered his question. He saw too much, and expected too much, and, dammit, he made her want too much. She tightened her arms around his neck and drew him down until they were nearly forehead to forehead. "Booker, if *you* want another shot at me, take it now. I've been hurting all night, thanks to you, and if you're not going to put me out of my misery, I'm going to take care of myself."

Desperation fueled the ultimatum. A risky move for a woman who didn't have a hell of a lot left except pride, but the glimpse of raw hunger in his eyes gave her hope. Then those eyes went dark and serious. "Welcome to my world, Jailbait. I've been suffering since you opened the door in two scraps of lace. Answer my question, and I'll put us both out of our misery."

Anger fanned flames already running through her blood. She'd had enough of people blackmailing her, be it her mom's classic brand or Booker's sexual brinksmanship, but she twined her fingers into his hair and swept her mouth over his in a deliberate torment as she uttered three words. "You. Wouldn't. Dare."

The next second strong hands cupped her jaw, capturing her, as his mouth slammed down on hers. A whole lot of heat, and need, and some barely banked male temper flowed into her mouth. She drank it down like a shot of whiskey, not caring about the burn.

And then it was gone. He stepped away so abruptly she would have fallen were it not for the door at her back. She swallowed her cry of surprise and blinked at his retreating form.

"See you around, Jailbait."

Chapter Nine

I've called you. I've texted you. What do I get for my efforts? Silence. Don't make me come over there…

Booker sighed at the screen of his phone. His mother rarely issued idle threats, but he planned to ignore the text anyway, because she wasn't the woman he wanted to see right now.

There's someone I want you to meet before your sister's wedding…

He slammed the front door behind him and threw his keys and phone on the narrow table he'd put there for the express purpose of saving himself the pain of searching for the damn things every morning. Too bad he couldn't resolve *other* pains quite so easily.

A week spent in a semi-constant state of blue balls surely set some kind of record. One he preferred not to hold, obviously, but it was what it was. The sound of his footfalls changed from hushed thuds on the refinished oak floor to distinct treads on the black-and-white octagonal tile in the kitchen. A rummage through his nearly empty fridge produced a cold beer. He twisted the cap off, took a long swallow, and considered his options.

Avoiding the cause of his torment hadn't helped—though it had proved easier than expected. A normal week of circulating through their town generally put him in Lauralie's path at some point, but without the bakery as her control center, her daily routine had become less predictable.

So much for seeing her around.

He flicked his beer cap into the trash and wandered to the large, arched window over the sink to stare at the view—just enough light left in the day to identify the outlines of Channel Islands in the distance, but nothing unique enough to distract him from his thoughts. They wandered to Lauralie whenever he didn't keep them on a leash, and that was bad enough. But his dreams? Those were impossible to control. His subconscious refused to wear a leash. It treated him to feverish and all too lifelike fantasies.

The longing went beyond a physical ache. He *missed* her. Not just her body, or the sex. He missed her smart mouth and her hard head. Over the better part of ten years she'd worked her way under his skin, and there was no quick, painless way of getting her out.

Even knowing this, he'd spent the last week fighting relentless urges to engineer things so he would, in fact, see her around. He resisted, in part because arranging a "coincidental" encounter involved resorting to stalker-ish shit like staking out her apartment, but in larger part because the ruse wouldn't work. They'd both know he *had* given in, and, frankly, weaseling a confrontation ran afoul of his ethics. If he caved, he'd at least do it in a straightforward way—come to her door, tell her she had five seconds to slam it in his face or prepare for the ride of her life, and then do his level best to fuck an answer out of her.

Did your mother's visit have anything to do with why I

woke up alone on New Year's Day?

Not necessarily a tough question, but one requiring some honest discussion. Unfortunately, as soon as he showed up on her doorstep, he lost any hope of having one. She'd know she could have him on her terms, subject to whatever limits she set, which meant this thing between them would never progress. She'd never voluntarily share her troubles or ask for help. So he'd wait her out, even if it killed him, and pray she blinked first...soon.

The beacon from the lighthouse a few miles down the coast cut through the foggy dusk, and the solitary signal seemed to cut through his internal turmoil to another truth he'd been trying to ignore. Denise Peterson hadn't trekked all the way to Montendio to wish her daughter a happy New Year. She wanted something. Something more than a ride to the train station. And whatever it was, it worried Lauralie. The hunted look on her face when Miranda had mentioned Denise confirmed as much. She didn't want to confide in him, but that didn't mean she didn't need help.

Screw staying strong. He put the half-finished beer on the counter, and retraced his steps to the front door. He'd try the storm-in-and-fuck-an-answer-out-of-her approach. As he snagged his keys from the hall table, someone knocked on his door.

And that's what you get for ignoring texts—your mother on your doorstep.

"I can't talk to you now. I'm on my way out," he said as he opened the door, and then stopped in his tracks.

Lauralie stood there in a slinky black T-shirt of a dress that clung in all the right places and ended high on her bare legs. Her hair tumbled away from her face in wild curls. Her upraised fist hung in the air between them.

The rush of blood to his cock was instantaneous and dangerously mind-numbing. Unfortunately, his words—

words she couldn't know weren't intended for her—had the opposite effect on her. Flashing blue eyes narrowed at him, but not before he caught a flicker of hurt in their depths. "Fine. Whatever." She spun on her heel. "I don't know what the fuck I'm doing here anyw—"

He caught her arm and swung her around. Momentum brought her up against his chest and he trapped her there with an arm around her waist. "Not you, Jailbait. I thought you were...it doesn't matter." This counted as her blinking first, he decided, and rewarded himself for his patience by giving her a detailed demonstration of exactly what the fuck she was doing there.

As soon as his lips touched hers, she lunged into him. A moan vibrated from deep in her throat and her fingers speared into his hair.

He hauled her inside, kicked the door shut, and then staggered a little as she started to climb him before he had both feet planted. He got them planted fast, and grabbed her ass to hold her in place while she wrapped her legs around his hips. The feel of her squirming against him ratcheted the pressure in his balls up to a dangerous level. Apparently she felt the pressure, too, because she tore her mouth away long enough to say, "Now," and then dove back into the kiss.

Hell yes, now. A single step brought him to the handiest surface available—the hall table—and a sweep of his arm sent his phone and keys clattering across the hardwood. Her purse hit the floor next, with a careless *thump*. He dropped her down on the narrow perch. Her breath whooshed out at the sudden impact. Before he could even think about apologizing, she surged toward him again, reaching for the front of his white, button-down shirt. One frantic tug later, buttons went flying, pinging into walls. Raining along the baseboards.

"Hurry," she reiterated, and proceeded to bestow hard little bites along his jaw. Her palms rushed down his chest, along his abs, and over the front of his jeans. Then it was his turn to lose his breath, because her quick fingers tore his fly open, shoved his underwear out of her way, and fisted his throbbing shaft. A hard tug dragged his balls over the teeth of his zipper.

"Jesus, Jailbait." He leaned in and pinned her against the wall, his hands on either side of her head. "This is a perfect example of you not understanding the risk inherent in your situation. I've missed you. I've wanted you constantly for the last week and you've denied us both out of sheer stubbornness. I'm in no shape to be toyed with. Keep it up, and this is going to be brutal. You'll feel it for the next week, no matter how many times I kiss it better."

Her chin came up. Temper or excitement—knowing her, a good dose of both—whipped color into her cheeks. "I need brutal. I've been in pain for a week and nothing relieves it."

Nothing? "What did you try?" The words scraped his throat like razors. If she answered with Jessie, or Scott, or any other name, he was going to have to kill an innocent man. When he'd walked away to let her stew in her own juices, he hadn't factored in the possibility of her turning elsewhere for relief.

"What?" she murmured against his throat, sounding both distracted and confused.

"What'd you try?" He shoved a hand under her dress, and raked the skirt up to her waist. Tunneling under the top, he snagged the front of her bra and dragged it down until her breasts spilled over the cups. Her high, tight nipples poked against the thin dress. A firm tug on one brought her upright like a soldier snapping to attention. "Answer me."

"Oh, God." She shook her head as her words dissolved into another moan.

She needed to be able to speak to answer his question, for both their sakes. He forced himself to release her nipple. She slouched against the wall, chest heaving, and parted her legs. The drenched triangle of red silk flashing him might as well have been a red flag, and he a bull.

He shoved the scrap down, grabbed her hips and pulled her to the edge of the table. While she scrambled for handholds along the lip, he hitched her ankles onto his shoulders. When he looked down at her again, round eyes stared back at him.

"Answer me, Lauralie." He gripped the base of his cock and slapped it between her thighs, hard enough to make them both groan.

The long muscles along the backs of her legs tightened, and she bowed away from the wall. "For the love of God, Booker put it in…"

"What didn't work?" He slapped the damp juncture again, and blinked away the haze blurring his vision.

"This didn't work." Eyes flashing, she slid her hand down her stomach and between her legs. The backs of her fingers kneaded his cock as she stroked herself. "No amount of this worked—no matter how hard I tried." She sounded genuinely aggrieved as she stroked faster. "My favorite setting on the massage showerhead didn't work. My vibrator *with* my favorite setting on the massage showerhead didn't work. Every part of me hurts, Booker. Especially here. So give me your goddamn cock, because you've ruined me for everything else."

Thank Christ. Her confession loosened the claw of jealousy gripping him, but did little to soothe his other painfully primitive instincts. The pain only had one cure. Make sure she knew beyond a shadow of a doubt there were no other avenues of relief for either of them, and there never would be. "You think you're ruined? Jailbait, the fact you kept me waiting for six fucking days tells me I haven't even begun to ruin you. But I will now."

Every muscle in his body tightened to make good on the

promise, until his last, functioning brain cell issued a reminder. Condom. All the way upstairs in his nightstand. *Fuck.*

He must have cursed aloud, or else she read his mind, because she stopped touching herself, and held onto the edge of the table with both hands. "There's no risk. Do it."

Common decency dictated he offer her an assurance as well, but the thought of being inside her without any barriers took precedence over conversation. She trusted him or she wouldn't allow him the privilege. He rewarded her trust with a table rattling thrust.

The intensity wrenched a cry out of her. She arched up to vertical, and clamped her hand over her sex, fingers forming a wide V where his girth strained the limits of her soft, tight center. Her mouth dropped open, and her head lolled back. "Oh, God. Don't…" She inhaled carefully. "…move."

He didn't so much as twitch a muscle, but even so the first quivering spasms of her orgasm hugged his shaft. He endured them.

Whimpers of gratitude accompanied her exhale, and then the whimpers drew out into moans as the quick flutters deepened to rhythmic squeezes all along the length of his cock. Not moving ceased to be an option. He grabbed her ass with both hands, and jerked her forward until her shoulders hit the wall. "Hang on to something, Jailbait." Long days spent craving this moment turned his voice to a growl. "I'm about to ruin you for good."

Then he began to move. The next minutes…hell…seconds blurred into a series of quick-fire sensory assaults. Muscles burned as he thrust with abandon. Her heels dug into his shoulders. His hips pounded her ass every time he slammed into her, forcing gusty groans from deep in her throat. The relentless beat of the table hitting the wall hammered his ears, telling him his attempt to ease up was an abject failure. His balls grew slick from the pleasure he pumped out of her with every thrust. Her groan broke into a cry as the climax ravaged her, and pulled him in, too. He sank his fingers in her hair and brought her face close enough he could feel her breath on his lips. Dark pupils went wide in glassy blue eyes, and days worth of suffering shot out of him in a long, annihilating stream.

"Jesus Christ, you've ruined me, too, Jailbait. If you ever put me through a week of waiting again, I warn you now, neither one of us will survive the reunion."

. . .

Little distractions slowly pierced the cloud of contentment surrounding her—the edge of the table digging into her back, her hamstrings stretching past the point of comfort, and her toes tingling from lack of circulation. Heavy exhales ruffled the hair at her temples. She pried her eyes open and confronted her foot, still propped high on Booker's shoulder, but now much closer to her face because he was crashed against the wall with his head next to hers.

Maybe she groaned, or wiggled—she honestly didn't know—but he murmured, "Give me a second, and I'll untangle us."

He might be the only thing holding her in place. If he moved, chances were good she'd slide to the floor in a boneless heap. "Don't let go. I'm pretty sure I'll fall…"

Or maybe you just don't want to be shown to the door yet, which is idiotic, because you got what you came for.

His low laugh tickled her neck. "I'm not going to let you go, Jailbait."

The laugh, the nickname—these things told her his offhand comment meant he could handle her deadweight—but for some sad reason her ear heard a deeper pledge in the statement. True to his word, he eased back with slow control, so neither she nor the table risked toppling. Then he commenced dragging his extremely effective cock out of her, and all she could do was moan at the thought of him leaving her empty again after so much incredible fullness. The prospect compelled her to do something she never did — cling. "No. Not yet."

Despite her outburst, he slid free. A hot trickle of moisture — his, hers, a combination of both — washed over parts of her still stinging from the aggressive friction they'd endured. God, her body literally wept for him. A late-breaking call for dignity had her struggling to close her legs, but he wrapped his hands around her thighs and held them open.

"Uh-uh. We're not done. I know it wasn't easy for you to swallow your pride and come here, but you needed me." He parted her thighs wider to expose the source of the need. "Now it's my responsibility to see to your needs — each and every one of them — and I take my responsibility very seriously. But my dick requires a few minutes of recovery time before it's of any further use. Luckily, I have other ways to take care of you."

Let him take care of you? Uh-uh. You take care of yourself.

Except she couldn't, when it came to this. Not anymore. She'd spent a long, uncomfortable week learning that lesson. Damn him.

And worse, he knew it. The corner of his mouth cocked up. "You're awfully quiet, Lauralie."

"I'm *not* quiet, I just…" *Have to find a way to retreat without looking like I'm retreating.* "I don't want to get in the way of any plans you had for tonight."

Without taking his eyes off her face, he swept his thumb down her crease, drawing another gush of moisture from her and then using the residual traces of their release to lubricate her. "I don't give a shit about plans." Before she could find her tongue to speak, he slowly massaged her pleasure-swollen flesh. Her neck muscles gave out and she rested her head against the wall.

"I give a shit about you," he went on, all the while circling and stroking, moving ever nearer to the knot of nerves already quickening at the prospect of his touch. "And because I do, I also give a shit about you answering my question. I'll make it as painless as possible, but you know that's part of the deal."

The pace of his movements never changed, but even so, a slippery rope of panic tightened around her throat. She needed to get the hell out of there, because when she'd driven over here tonight, she hadn't thought past trying to have her way with him. Instead, he was doing it again. Saying things that knocked her off balance, and made her want to hold him closer and run away at the same time. "Booker—"

"Right after you scream my name as I give you your third orgasm of the night."

The oxygen-starved feeling subsided. His reprieve, coupled with the cocky tone in his voice restored her equilibrium. "Third? I don't know how you're counting, Sheriff."

He nudged her clit with the pad of his thumb, and sent warning flares shooting through her abdomen. "That's a load of crap. This is your third. Three more and you owe me breakfast tomorrow morning."

"You're counting chickens before they hatch." The tension was back, building between her legs, making her edgy.

"Am I?" He swept his thumb over her clit, again and again. She arched up as he increased the speed. His touch electrified her.

"Oh, God. Maybe not. Booker...don't stop." She started to tremble. "I'm going to come."

"You owe me a week's worth and I intend to collect every one of them."

Then he dropped a long, slow kiss on her lips, and it felt like a pledge, or a vow, or something else she shouldn't be so ready to hold onto. She wasn't looking for promises, dammit. But another slick slide of his thumb, and he delivered on one anyway. She went flying, body spiraling out of control, yet somehow the storm of sensations calmed her chaotic thoughts—like the moment of clarity in the eye of a hurricane.

He's promised you sex. Amazing sex. But still, just sex. Nothing you can't handle.

Chapter Ten

Scents of aftershave and Tide pods filled her nose, and told Laurie the sheets she lay face down across didn't belong to her. The pillow under her cheek? Also not hers. Likewise the blanket crumpled around her ankles. She cracked her eyes open and confirmed her worst suspicions. Despite her firm plan not to, she'd spent the night in Booker's bed. How had it happened? Or, more to the point, *why* had she allowed it to happen?

He'd carted her to his bedroom after "taking care of her" in the hall, and she'd been too limp and satisfied to do anything except go along for the ride. Later, after he'd given her a thorough tour of his big, sturdy bed and a convincing demonstration of his ten minute rebound time, she'd feigned sleep, thinking she'd make her way home after he drifted off.

Only it had been she who drifted off, and woken up in the wee hours of the morning to find her wrists handcuffed together, and Booker sleeping beside her with a smile on his face. The cuffs made it impossible for her to dress, much less drive, but as those realizations were sinking in Booker woke up just enough to show her the shackles didn't impair her ability to have a screaming orgasm. Not in the least. Afterward, as she'd floated on the fringes of sleep, he'd murmured, "You owe me breakfast."

Her hands weren't cuffed together anymore, but—she raised her head an inch off the pillow—sure enough, last night's accessory still encircled one wrist.

And where the hell was the sheriff of O-town this morning? She usually didn't out-sleep anyone—running a bakery made for early mornings—but today it seemed Booker had gotten the jump on her. The whole house was silent. She rolled over and pulled the sheet up to her chest. A folded, white piece of paper sat like a tiny tent on his nightstand, and a sick little twinge tugged her stomach. Was he giving her a dose of her own medicine? Teaching her what it felt like to wake up alone in someone else's bed with a note saying *See you around*?

Early indications hinted it sucked. But she was a big girl, and she had it coming. With a sigh, she lifted the note and flipped it open.

Went to the store. Behave yourself while I'm gone and I'll give you a chance to earn your clothes back by making me breakfast.

Yeah, right. Where was she supposed to go with a handcuff dangling from her wrist, and—she glanced at the empty spot on the dark blue rug where she last remembered seeing her dress—no clothes. Despite the sarcastic thoughts, a smile tugged at her lips.

She bounced off the bed and shrugged into the large, white terrycloth bathrobe he'd slung across the back of one of the two leather chairs in the sitting area of his spacious bedroom. Of course he hadn't. Escape was *her* MO. It's not like he had a crazy mother prone to show up at the worst possible moments and make his life hell.

Stop. Don't let Denise spoil the best morning you've had in over a week.

Absolutely not. Her mother was two hundred miles away, and not likely to come around anytime soon, considering Laurie didn't have anything left to leech away.

The thought offered bitter comfort. She cruised downstairs in search of something more inspiring—like coffee. As she passed the entryway, a thump on the other side of the front door slowed her down. Either Booker was back or he'd forgotten something.

She twisted the knob and swung the door open. "Kidnapping my clothes is…"

The rest of her sentence died on her tongue. Rebecca Booker stood on the threshold, tall and toned with her dark hair smoothed into her signature chin-length bob. She wore a coordinated yoga outfit and held a bag of produce from the farmer's market. Her smile faded as she blinked at the stranger answering her son's door. Then one dark, arched brow rose in a feminine version of an expression Laurie associated with Booker.

"Mrs. Booker…"

"Sorry." The cool, slightly amused word conveyed many things, but sorrow wasn't among them. "You have the advantage. I was looking for my son." She took a step back and gestured to the doorway. "This is definitely his house, and that"—she indicated the robe Laurie wore—"is definitely the present I got him for Christmas, but you I don't recognize."

"I'm Laurie. I'm just…" *The maid? The plumber?* Nope. There was no plausible way to end the sentence. "…a friend. Um, he's not home right now, but he'll be back shortly. Would you like to come in and wait? Here, let me take that." She reached out for the bag of groceries. The movement sent the handcuffs sliding down her wrist, until the empty loop dangled from the sleeve of the robe. It swung there, hypnotically, while sunlight glinted on the metal.

Shit.

Now both of his mother's eyebrows disappeared behind meticulously maintained bangs. Her lips twitched before she firmed them into a neutral line. "I'd better take a rain check. Here…sustenance." She handed over the bag of groceries. "If I know my son, he doesn't have a thing in his fridge except day old pizza and domestic beer."

Laurie nodded and accepted the bag, though in truth she couldn't confirm his mother's comment, as she'd never set foot in the kitchen, much less looked in the fridge. Admitting her realm of knowledge extended only from the entryway table to Booker's bedroom wouldn't improve the situation.

Not that Rebecca needed rescuing. She simply smiled again, and said, "Lovely to meet you, Laura." A bouncy pivot sent her gliding down the walkway toward the silver Tesla parked at the curb. "Please tell Booker to call me when he has a moment."

She bit back the automatic impulse to correct her name, and closed the door. Rebecca Booker did not need to know the correct name of her son's current fuck-buddy — and that's all this would end up amounting to, because this morning's encounter landed her squarely in the category of girl-you-don't-take-home-to-mother.

You certainly didn't try to pass her off as the love of your life. She carried the groceries to the kitchen and hefted the bag onto the counter. He was probably getting an earful from his mom right now about the tramp who'd answered his door in a bathrobe and handcuffs. She unloaded organic tomatoes with unnecessary force. He'd dump her fake-girlfriend ass as soon as he got home.

Fine. Whatever. It hardly mattered anymore, anyway. She'd spoken to Chelsea yesterday and found out the bonus looked iffy. The insurance company was burying her with paperwork. Her financial rescue was unraveling from all sides. She snagged a package of locally grown oranges from the bag, tearing the netting in the process. The fruit bounced on the counter, rolled in every direction, and spilled onto the floor.

So what are you doing here?

Excellent question.

. . .

Booker came in quietly, in case his guest still slept, but stopped short at the kitchen entry when a fist-sized missile flew past his head.

He dodged, and the object thumped into the hallway. Lauralie stood in the middle of the kitchen, ready to hurl another orange at him.

"Someone really needs her morning coffee."

The comment earned him an angry little scream, and then the next orange zoomed at him—on a much lower trajectory this time. He used the grocery bag he carried to block it, preferring to risk breaking the half-dozen eggs he'd just bought than his balls.

While she bent to scoop another orange off the floor, he put his bag on the counter next to a half-unloaded one he had a pretty good suspicion who to thank for, and closed the distance. She straightened, and he got a full blast of glaring blue eyes and fiery cheeks before he caught her wrist to prevent her from taking a close-range shot.

"Before you damage parts of me we're both fond of, want to tell me why you're fired up?"

"Let go."

"Hell, no. Talk to me."

"Booker, if you don't let go of me right now, I swear to God I'm going to—don't you dare…"

He did dare. He took the dangling end of the handcuff

and locked it around his wrist. "Let's try this again. Talk. To. Me."

"This"—she rattled the chain connecting their wrists—"isn't funny."

"Depends on your perspective."

Her chin tipped up. "Call your mom. Ask her if she found it funny when she stopped by this morning."

He tamped down on the urge to wince, and shrugged a shoulder instead. "I don't know how funny she thought it was, but I'll bet she realizes she needs to call before she drops by."

"You're not funny, either. Me, answering your door wearing your bathrobe and these stupid, freaking"—she rattled the chain on the handcuffs—"things, tells your mother in fairly explicit terms we slept together last night—"

"As it happens, we did sleep together last night."

"Don't get cute. It sends the wrong kind of message. It completely torpedoes your plan."

"No. It tells her we're involved. How does that undermine my plan?"

"You seriously don't understand?"

Oh, he understood. But did she? The situation pissed her off because she actually gave a damn what his mother thought of her. She'd invested more than her pride. She *cared*. Which meant they weren't standing on such uneven ground after all, but he knew better than to enjoy the revelation right now. "Look"—he grabbed a handful of the front of the robe and tugged her closer, even though she stiffened—"I get that this wasn't the most traditional first impression, but I don't always know when my mom is going to show up on my doorstep. Maybe you can relate?"

She shook her head. "When it comes to mothers, we have nothing in common. Trust me."

"Enlighten me. Tell me about the last time your mom paid an unannounced call."

Those blue eyes drifted to his and then bounced away. "New Year's Day. She showed up on my patio at dawn, and yes, she's the reason you woke up alone that morning. I got dressed, and got her gone before she could do any damage."

He wrapped his free arm around her waist, and pulled her closer. "What kind of damage would she do?"

"Make a scene." She sighed and sagged against him. "Embarrass me. Embarrass you…"

"I'm not easily embarrassed, Jailbait. You shouldn't be either. She may embarrass herself, but it's got nothing to do with you."

"Says the man standing in the shelter of a respectable family tree."

"Those limbs cast a shadow—not one I'm ashamed of, most of the time—but I've worked hard to establish my own reputation, and be judged by my own accomplishments. I extend the same courtesy. Nothing your mother says or does impacts my view of you. I draw conclusions about people based on who they are, not the names listed on their birth certificate." He let the words sink in for a moment, then asked, "What did your mother want?"

"Same thing she always wants. Money." A hard laugh punctuated the statement. Two angry slashes of red stained her cheeks. "I hadn't seen her in a year and a half, and she showed up on New Year's Day to shake me down."

"How much did you give her?"

She replied after the barest of pauses. "Nothing."

"Nothing?"

She stared at a point over his shoulder. "I gave her a ride to the train station. Of course she lifted the forty bucks I had in my wallet somewhere along the way, but really, that's on me. I should have seen it coming."

He could see she was holding something back. He knew the signs—guarded tone of voice, rigid spine, pulse fluttering at the base of her throat. But he didn't press. Maybe it had been more than forty dollars, or her mom had helped herself to a credit card, too. Whatever it was, it was done. His heart broke for her. She'd gotten a raw deal in the family department. "Idiot," he said, knowing she'd recognize sarcasm when she heard it.

"Yeah. I'm a fucking idiot." She blew out a breath and gave him a tired smile. "That's what she loves about me."

He tightened his arm and drew her against him. There was much to love about her, and the fact that her mother has always been too wrapped up in her own selfish dramas to realize it made Denise Peterson the fucking idiot. "The only idiotic thing you do is think you need to deal with her on your own."

She didn't. Not as long as he had anything to say about it.

"Booker, she's my mom, which makes her my problem."

"That's not true. If she shows up at your home or business and causes a scene, she's disturbing the peace and that makes her my problem. If she refuses to leave, she's trespassing. Again, my problem. Likewise if she steals from you. You're not responsible for her, and you're not the right person to deal with her. The next time she contacts you, let me know, okay?"

She blinked up at him, clearly taken aback by the request. "I—all right."

"Good. When it comes to family, nobody should have to go it alone. Including me. Are you free tomorrow night?"

"Yes." Belatedly, she shot him a cautious look. "Why?"

"Date number two."

"Have you lost your mind? Booker, I don't think this dating thing is going to—"

"Fine. Don't think of it as a date."

She tipped her head. "What should I think of it as?"

"A chance to meet my mother wearing something other than handcuffs and a bathrobe."

Chapter Eleven

Laurie cracked the passenger-side window of Booker's car and lifted her face to the cool air, trying not to let the winding cobblestone driveway and claustrophobic canopy of bougainvillea turn her nervous flutters into a case of carsickness. Just then the driveway widened, and flattened, and the red-tiled, multi-tiered roofline of a massive Mediterranean-style villa rose into view. The bottom dropped out of her stomach.

"Jesus, your parents are rich."

Booker stared ahead, concentrating on the drive, but inclined his head. The crisp, white collar of his dress shirt skimmed his neck, setting off his sun-bronzed skin and the dark blue of his suit jacket. "They manage." He steered along the circling path to the front of the mansion and parked behind a line of vehicles that might just as easily have been showcased at some luxury car dealership. "Big or small, it's still just a house." He turned off the engine, and got out of the car.

She blew out a breath, wiped her damp palms on the skirt

of her little black dress, and stepped out as well, almost running into him as he came around to open her door. Whoops. Her etiquette sucked. She took a tiny step back, and smoothed her dress. "Are you sure I look okay?"

Granted, she'd asked the question at least ten times since he'd arrived on her doorstep, and apparently he was tired of replying, because he took her by the waist, backed her up against the car, and leaned his lower body into hers. The hard jut of his erection branded her hip. "I sense you're nervous, Jailbait. Does this help alleviate your worries?"

In a strange way, it did. The primitive demonstration stabilized some unsteady place inside her, but the immediate rush of her body's equally primitive response promised an uncomfortable evening if she didn't get herself under control. She gave him an utterly ineffective shove. "Put that away, unless you're prepared to skip the party and use it."

"Uh-uh. You don't earn it until after the party. Stay by my side for the next two hours. Talk weddings with my sister, smile and nod while my mother tells you how to live your life. Laugh at my dad's jokes." He lowered his head and nipped her earlobe. "But if at any time during the evening your nerves start to get the better of you, just give me a signal. I'll find a private spot"—he pressed his cock against her again—"and alleviate your worries a little more."

Without waiting for a reply, he stepped back, took her hand, and led her into the house. She walked into the party on shaky legs, but now it had nothing to do with nerves.

Kate spied them first, and made her way over, looking sleek in an emerald green dress. As she closed in, she snagged a brawny guy with a shaved head, a ginger beard, and a few hundred dollars worth of silver piercing his ears. All of it completely at odds with his tailored suit. Kate hugged Booker, and then, while he and Sons of Anarchy shook hands, Kate hugged her as well.

Surprise froze her for a moment, but Kate didn't seem to notice. She drew away and gestured to the burly guy. "I'm so happy to see you again. Laurie, meet my fiancé, Aaron."

Okay, that brought more surprise. Aaron looked nothing like she expected. His off-center grin said he knew it. "Nice to officially meet you. I crashed your New Year's Eve party, briefly, but this gent neglected to make introductions."

"I had other priorities on New Year's Eve," Booker replied, sounding not at all sorry.

"I know. I've got the Amex bill to prove it."

"You can't put a price on happiness."

"You *can* put a price on a round of drinks for a pub full of people. It's a thousand dollars, plus tip. Speaking of introductions…" His green eyes swung back to her. "I heard you met Rebecca."

"Aaron!" Kate elbowed him in the rib.

"What?" He rubbed his side. "That was the most blinding meet-the-mum story I ever heard."

Was it possible for her head to spontaneously combust? She glared at Booker.

"I didn't say a word."

"Mom told us," Kate explained, and then lost her battle with a giggle. "And yes, for the record, you definitely win for most epic meet-the-mom story. If it's any consolation, she said you had good manners, and admirable composure. Also, she was happy to see her Christmas gift hadn't ended up in the back of the closet."

Just as she wished for the polished tile to part and swallow her up, a familiar voice called from across the room.

"Booker!"

Laurie looked over to see Rebecca winding her way through the large room. A tall, dark-suited man with Booker's straight nose and strong jawline followed. His father.

"What a surprise. So nice of you to fit us into your

schedule," his mother said as she accepted a hug and kiss on the cheek from her son.

"I'm not sure why you're surprised, Mom. I told you I'd be here," he replied, and leaned forward to hug his father.

"Yes, but one never knows, with that job of yours."

Booker rolled his eyes, and then put his hand at Laurie's back. "Mom, Dad, I'd like you to meet—"

Rebecca turned to her and recognition flickered across her face. "Laura. We met yesterday."

"Lauralie," Booker corrected.

"Laurie," she interjected. "Please call me Laurie."

Mr. Booker extended a hand. "Call me Richard. Sounds like you already know Rebecca."

"Yes." She shook his hand and nodded to Booker's mom. "Nice to see you again."

"Likewise. I'm delighted Booker brought you tonight. We didn't get much of a chance to talk yesterday, since you were a bit…tied up."

Har. Har. Striving for the high road, she smiled. "I'm a big fan of Best Life's sunscreen. Use it every day."

Rebecca beamed. "I love to talk to fans of the brand. Tell me, Laurie, what do you do?"

She really needed to work out a pat answer to this question. "I'm kind of…figuring out my next move, professionally."

"Oh. Did you recently graduate?"

Kate tried to help by explaining. "Laurie owned Babycakes, Mom."

Rebecca's brows drew together. "Babycakes?"

"A bakery," Laurie supplied.

Her forehead smoothed. She pressed a hand to her chest, and laughed. "That explains why I'm clueless. Best Life is a health-conscious brand, and I'm the face of it, so I try to avoid temptation. Offering our customers positive, nourishing ways to enhance life has always been an integral part of our mission statement."

Of course it was. Selling sugary carbs probably ranked right up there with dealing crack in Rebecca Booker's estimation. Hell, she might as well have worn a bathrobe and handcuffs tonight, because despite her little black dress and counterfeit pearls, she still came off as an outsider. A tacky outsider. She dredged up a smile and tried for a breezy reply. "I guess it's a good thing Babycakes isn't around to tempt you."

Nope. Not breezy. Awkward.

And Rebecca picked up on it. "I wouldn't go that far. My willpower works, most of the time, but when it weakens, I bolster myself with a treat from the new line of organic dark chocolates we're launching. Be sure to try them." She pointed to the table set up in one corner of the room. "We use only fair-trade cocoa, and don't pollute the flavor with a bunch of sugar or other additives. The end result is pure, luxurious chocolate loaded with antioxidants, and—"

"Mom, it's a party, not a product meeting," Kate said.

Rebecca laughed. "I'm not going to apologize. You know how passionate I am about Best Life." She zeroed in on Laurie and added, "People should spend their energy doing what fulfills them. Did you get burned-out on running your own business, or…?"

The unconsciously ironic question shattered her brittle self-control. Inappropriate and slightly hysterical laughter burst out of her. Everybody in the vicinity glanced her way, including Miranda McQueen and a clutch of her cronies, who turned up their sculpted noses and whispered behind their hands. She could practically hear the commentary. *Her? She's nobody. Booker's Nido Terrace sex toy, thinking she's going to elevate her status.*

Booker slid an arm around her shoulder before saying, "The bakery burned down New Year's Day."

"Oh, dear." Concern filled Rebecca's eyes. "I hope nobody was hurt."

The words served as a reminder of how much worse things could have been, and helped dispel her laughter. "Thankfully, no. We were closed for the holiday. I was lucky."

Rebecca nodded, and opened her mouth to respond, but her attention snagged on something over Booker's shoulder, and her gaze sharpened. "Uh-oh. Aunt Sarah is sipping her second cocktail and circling the bartender like a shark. Richard, we'd better get over there."

"I'm on it. Nice to meet you, Laurie."

"Have fun," Rebecca directed the rest of them, as she turned to follow her husband. "Don't forget to try the chocolate. Oh, and Laurie, be sure to find me before you leave. I have something for you."

"Sure," she replied, a little thrown by the request, although Rebecca walked away like a woman accustomed to people doing as she asked. Laurie slowly exhaled and eyed Booker. "*That* went well."

Aaron laughed. "Are you kidding? That was brilliant. I made the mistake of wearing a leather jacket the first time I met Rebecca—which also happened to be my first day on the job at Best Life. By the time she'd finished her animal rights lecture I wanted to curl up into a fetal position on the conference room floor and cry."

"You grew to love her," Kate insisted, and took his hand.

He lifted their joined hands, and kissed hers. "I grew to love *you*. Rebecca, Richard, and this tosser just happen to come part and parcel."

"Aw. Isn't he sweet?" Kate wrapped her arms around Aaron's neck, went up on her tiptoes, and kissed him.

"And now I want to curl up into a fetal position and cry," Booker said drily, and pulled her toward the other side of the room. "Welcome to my nightmare, Jailbait. Can I get you a drink?"

"Absolutely. But point me to the powder room first." She needed a moment to fortify her armor before she circulated, in part because she found Rebecca Booker's attitude hard to pin down. She'd prepared for the three D's—disapproval, distrust, and disdain—and instead she'd gotten…well… she didn't know. And the uncertainty unnerved her. Booker directed her toward a hallway, told her "Second door on the right," and kissed her soundly. She staggered off with the heat from his lips tingling on hers.

The powder room door opened as she approached, and she ended up face-to-face with Miranda. The woman looked at her like something that crawled out of an alley. "Oh my, if it isn't the baker. How…interesting to see you here."

This attitude she knew well enough, and she refused to let the old blueblood intimidate her. She crossed her arms and cocked her hip. "I always try to be interesting."

"I'm sure you do. And I'm sure, in some circles, you're positively fascinating."

Whatever. Figuratively speaking, she had an engraved invitation to this thing, and she wasn't above waving it in the stuck-up bitch's face. "Booker seems to think so."

Miranda's lips pressed into a grim smile. "Men's interests can be so predictable, can't they? And predictably short-lived once they satisfy their curiosity, but I suspect you already know, given your pedigree." Hard blue eyes gleamed with satisfaction as she brushed past Laurie. "Enjoy your evening."

It will be your last at an event like this. The unspoken words taunted her as vividly as the iconic red soles of the stilettos gracing the older woman's feet. Each step sent a dismissive echo reverberating down the hallway. Laurie ducked into the powder room and faced her reflection in the gilded mirror at the same time she faced a few facts.

Fact one: Miranda had, essentially, nailed it. Once her six-date commitment to Booker ended, they ended. He'd offered her a deal. Nothing more. The side benefits, *interesting* as they were, didn't change that fundamental truth. He needed her as a short-term diversion.

Fact two: she couldn't let herself forget fact one, because if she did, she might just—the carsick feeling returned in full force—fall in love with him.

Don't. She used a tissue to blot her forehead and tried to calm her churning stomach with a heaping dose of reality. *You care for him. He means more to you than any man ever has, but don't fall in love. You're not wired for it. You don't believe in forever, remember? Booker does, and he deserves forever with someone who fits the brand, and has the pedigree, and, most importantly, doesn't have an ugly skeleton in her closet.*

She flipped the tap on full blast to drown out her thoughts, and held her hands under cool water. It helped. After a moment she turned off the tap and risked another look in the mirror…and faced one more fact.

He didn't ask you for forever. He asked you for six dates. Get out there and do what he's counting on you to do.

Right. After drying her hands, she opened the door, and stepped into the hallway—directly into Booker's mother.

"Oh, how perfect. You're just the person I hoped to find."

"Me?"

"Yes. Come with me." Rebecca took off down the hall, away from the party, and motioned for Laurie to follow. "This won't take long. I have something for you. Something you'll find very useful, I think."

Great. Was Rebecca going to write her a check to get her out of Booker's life? If so, the woman sure was chipper when it came to bribery. She led them to a sleekly feminine office and stepped over to a small, round table with a Best Life shopping bag sitting on the smooth, glass surface.

"When Booker told me he was bringing you tonight, I

took the liberty of curating some selections from one of our in-development product lines. This is all very top secret." She reached into the bag and pulled out a box with the scrolled, gold Best Life logo across the lid and held it out to Laurie. "I don't want to sound too much like a proud spokeswoman, but I know you'll find we hit the right balance between authenticity, elegance, and comfort."

Laurie reached for the slim, rectangular box. It felt light and insulated, and…valuable. "Mrs. Booker, I'm flattered—"

"Call me Rebecca. We should be on a first name basis."

She had next to no experience with mother-of-the-boyfriend relationships, but this one seemed to be moving awfully fast. "Rebecca, I'm flattered you thought of me, but—"

"But nothing. I see an opportunity to improve something, I take it." Anticipation sparkled in Rebecca's eyes. "Go ahead. Open it."

The lid lifted off easily. Inside was a white, suede clamshell box with the same embossed gold letters across the top. The kind of box a jeweler might use to hold a necklace or bracelet. "Really Mrs. Booker, you—"

Rebecca reached over and flipped up the lid.

"Shouldn't have," Laurie uttered as she stared at the polished silver handcuffs nestled in white silk. Holy crap, Booker's mother was giving her Best Life bondage gear.

"I just couldn't help myself!" Rebecca lifted the cuffs out of the box. "These are sterling silver, hypoallergenic"—she pressed a trigger and opened one cuff—"velvet-lined, and best of all"—she pressed another trigger to open the second cuff—"they have these handy little release buttons, so you'll never get stuck. I think the market will go crazy for them, don't you?"

"I—I don't know what to say." Inappropriate was the only word that sprang to mind.

Rebecca laughed. "Look at you, blushing. Please. There's

nothing to be embarrassed about. My children are adults, and I know they have sex. I'd be worried if they didn't. After all, a satisfying sex life is integral to health and happiness. Why wouldn't I support that?"

She hoped it was a rhetorical question because she couldn't come up with a proper response. Nothing in her admittedly limited etiquette handbook covered this scenario. *Just take the gift, say thank you, and get the hell out of here before things get really—ha—off the chain.* "Well, um…thank you. They look very…durable." *Shit.*

"They are. Those beauties will hold up to anything. And I do mean anything. Best Life puts every product we develop through rigorous testing."

"That's…" She shut the box, fit the lid back on top, and struggled for a word to get her out of this encounter without further discussion on the merits of fancy handcuffs. "…reassuring. Thanks again, for the, uh, thoughtful gift." With that graceless stammering hanging in the air, she took a step away from the table.

"Wait." Rebecca offered the bag. "Don't forget the rest."

"The rest?" Laurie's arm went on autopilot, and she watched like a spectator as Booker's mom looped the silk cords of the bag handle around her outstretched fingers.

"I'm planning to market this as a kit. We've put together all the essentials. Some organic massage oil, a few naturally flavored gels, and some other goodies." She winked at Laurie. "We want to keep things interesting."

Interesting. There was that word again. She managed a smile and another thank you, and then made her way back to the party, wondering if everyone she passed was secretly thinking, *Get a load of the interesting girl Booker brought, and her interesting bag of tricks.*

Booker appeared out of nowhere, and handed her a glass of wine. "I was about to send out a search party."

She took a swallow, but her mouth went dry as she looked at him. The uniform had always done it for her, but tonight he was walking, talking, broad-shouldered suit porn. Corporate America had missed out big time when Booker had opted for law enforcement over a corner office. "I got waylaid. Said hello to your good friend, Miranda, and then had a chat with your mother."

"Busy girl. What's in the bag?"

"I don't want to tell you, and you don't want to know. Let's just say your mom is committed to your health and happiness."

His eyes narrowed on the bag, and then flicked to her. She raised a brow.

"You're right. I don't want to know. Feel like getting some fresh air?" He shrugged his jacket off. The sight of him in his tailored, white shirt did ridiculous things to her hormones, and shoved a whole lot of her earlier crazy to the back of her mind. *Don't overcomplicate things. You're two consenting adults with a mutual attraction. Nothing could be simpler.*

"Fresh air isn't really what I'm in the mood for right now." She turned so she faced him and rested a hand on his chest. Beneath his shirt, his heart beat strong and steady. "Remember what you promised me if I came in here and played nice with your family?"

His eyes darkened and his hand strayed to the small of her back. "I do."

"Did I earn it?"

"Hell yes. Any way you want it, for as long as you can take it."

• • •

"Oh my God. No more. I can't take it," Lauralie moaned into the pillow she hugged, and dug her heels into his collarbones in a halfhearted attempt to pull away. He clamped his hands around her waist, and used his tongue to prove her wrong. She took it, and took it, until the momentum of her orgasm lifted her body almost completely off the bed. A few pulsing seconds later she collapsed onto the mattress.

"I think I'm paralyzed. I can't feel anything from the waist down."

He dislodged one foot from his shoulder, and kissed the arch. "Feel that?"

"Um…I'm not sure."

"How about this?" He kissed the inside of her knee.

Her lips curved into a smile. "Hmm. Nope," she replied, not bothering to open her eyes.

"Time for extraordinary measures." He flipped her over, and bit her ass.

She shrieked, and struggled to get her knees under her. "Booker…!"

"Hey, look at that. You're cured." He released her and ducked to avoid her foot as she scrambled across the bed. "It's a miracle."

A pillow sailed over and bounced off his chest. "It's a miracle you didn't get kicked in the head."

He eased onto the bed, staying low. "Fortune favors the bold." Because it was there, he brushed his lips over her ankle, and then drew away and ran his thumb over the small, smooth dents of the two triangle shaped scars.

She stiffened for a moment, as if realizing he inspected the scars. He looked at her, not surprised to see wary blue eyes focused on him. "Surfing?"

"I don't remember. They've always been there."

He kissed the old wounds again. They'd spent the evening with his family, so he'd deliberately brought them back to her place, where she'd feel most comfortable. Her turf. Her bed. Her safe zone. If he couldn't get an honest answer out of her now, they were doomed. "You have an excellent memory, Lauralie."

She stayed silent so long he almost prompted her again, but then she said, "When I was little—like four or five—my mom took me with her one afternoon while she visited her *friend* Bob." She made air quotes around the word.

"Uncle Bob?" He deliberately kept the question light, although muscles tightened in his gut.

"Ha. Nobody stuck around long enough to earn uncle status. Anyway, this particular friend had a huge house and big backyard complete with pool, spa, sports court—the works. He also had a big Doberman. I think it usually had the run of the yard, but since we were there he put it in the fenced area around the pool. My mom told me play in the yard until she came back."

"She left a four year old unsupervised?" It wasn't really a question. They'd never talked about it before, but even on the night they met, he'd understood Denise hadn't suddenly checked out as a mom when Lauralie turned sixteen. Still, hearing such a bald-faced example of neglect triggered protective instincts over twenty years too late to do her any good.

Lauralie stared at the ceiling, but her lips twisted into a tight smile. "I learned to look out for myself at an early age."

He gently tapped her scarred ankle. "But?"

"But, I was kicking this little soccer ball around the yard, and I kicked it too hard. It sailed over the fence surrounding the pool, bounced a few times, and rolled to a stop about a foot short of the gate. The dog was at the other end of the enclosure, and it stood when I approached the gate, but it didn't make any sounds. The ball was right there. I figured I could stick my foot through the posts and use my foot to roll it closer, then reach in and grab it. As soon as tried, I found myself playing tug-a-war against a snarling Doberman latched onto my ankle. I screamed bloody murder, and between that and the dog growling, Denise and Uncle Bob came running. Lucky for me, the dog let go as soon as it got the command. Lucky for Denise, Uncle Bob was loaded, and forked over a wad of cash to forget the whole unfortunate incident ever happened."

Hot, useless rage burned through him, but he held it in check because it wouldn't do her any good now. He couldn't stop himself from brushing his thumb over the marks. "Have you heard from her since New Year's?"

"Nope."

"Jailbait?" He waited until her eyes flicked his way. "Tell me if she contacts you."

"The odds are low."

"I didn't ask for the odds. I asked you to tell me if she contacts you."

She rolled over and settled her chin on her folded arms. He interpreted the move easily enough. She wanted this conversation to be over.

"Okay."

"Thank you." Tight muscles in his gut relaxed a measure. He couldn't protect her when she'd been a kid, but he could protect her now. He kissed his way up her body.

"No more scars," he murmured when he reached the nape of her neck.

"No. I learned to guard myself better."

Correction. No more visible scars. Hers were the kind most people couldn't see. And he had to be careful with them. He moved to the head of the bed, and pulled her into his arms. She let him gather her close.

Looking to change the topic to something less heavy, he asked, "Why baking?"

She moved her head to where his chest met his shoulder, and snuggled into the hollow. "I like the smell of goodies fresh out of the oven. Who doesn't?"

"Um. My mom? I can honestly say we didn't have that smell in our house very often growing up."

Her fingertips drew lazy swirls over his chest. "Me neither, actually. Denise's cooking skills extended to cereal, canned soup, and frozen dinners. She wasn't going to bake a cake for my birthday, or make cupcakes for the school fundraiser."

Somehow the conversational road led back to the place he'd been trying to steer them out of. Before he could try again, she went on.

"The first time I ever had a home-cooked anything was at Chelsea's sixth birthday party. Denise dropped me off way early because she had plans, and I remember walking into the house and smelling something amazing. If happiness had a scent, it was coming from Chelsea's kitchen. Her mom was baking her cake—chocolate, with chocolate frosting. I sat in their kitchen with my little mouth watering, thinking life would be awesome if I could smell that smell every day." Her hand stilled on his chest. "I did, for awhile, and it *was* awesome."

He threaded his fingers through hers and kissed her temple. "You will again, soon."

"We'll see." Doubt clouded the words. "The insurance company is still doing their investigation. Chelsea's bonus looks iffy."

"You know I'm loaded, right?"

"We've been over this. I'm not taking any money from you other than what comes as part of our deal. Besides, investing in a bakery would be awkward for you."

"Why is that?"

"Babycakes doesn't suit the Best Life brand."

"*I'm* not part of the Best Life brand. I never have been. I'm my own man, Jailbait."

She patted his hand. "Booker, you're part of the brand

just by breathing."

The comment set off a flare of annoyance inside him. He tamped it down because she'd just spent the evening immersed in his family, listening to his mom preach the Best Life gospel. Best Life wasn't *his* life, but he understood why the distinction might be blurry for her about now.

He could afford a little patience.

Chapter Twelve

"What's the word from Maui?"

Laurie held her phone to her ear with her shoulder while she unlocked her apartment.

"A cautious thumbs up," Chelsea replied from the other end of the phone. "I had meetings this week to try and resolve the snag I told you about in the sale of the hotel. The parties reached an agreement, in concept. Nothing's final until the contracts are signed, but I wanted to let you know my bonus is back within the realm of possibility."

Hope expanded in Laurie's chest. "I can't thank you enough for what you're doing." She walked into her apartment, shut the door behind her, and then absently picked up the silver commuter mug Booker had left on the end table on his way out that morning. Somehow, spending last weekend together had evolved into spending *every* night of the past week together, and as a result she had a little collection of Booker's stuff at her place: the coffee cup, a six pack of his favorite beer in her fridge, a dark blue Montenido Sheriff's Dept. sweatshirt that smelled like him — and swam on her, but she had commandeered it anyway.

"Save the thanks until I come through with the money."
She stopped and cleared her throat. "Like I said, the deal's
not done until the deal's done, but things look decent."

"You sound tired." She put her purse on the kitchen
counter, along with Booker's mug, and leaned on the opposite
counter.

"I'm okay. A little tired. I've been working a lot."

Guilt gnawed at her. "No bonus is worth your health."

"Don't worry, Mom. I'm fine. Any word from the insurance
company?"

Laurie sensed the deflection beneath the sarcasm, but she
went with the subject change because she actually couldn't
mother Chelsea from this distance. "I spoke with the adjuster
today. They have my itemized claim, and they received the
report from the Montenido fire inspector, which states the
cause was an electrical short."

"So, that's good, right? They should be able to process
your claim soon?"

"God forbid they be that up-front. They've got their own
investigator, who still has to submit *his* report, but as long as
it raises no, quote 'new information or questions,' I should be
good to go."

"Great. That means they'll issue payment soon. What
new information or questions would there be? An electrical
short caused a fire that resulted in a total loss of your business.
End of story."

*Information like I stopped by the bakery that morning,
and emptied my safe?* "I have no idea."

"I know this is impossible, but try not to stress about it.
How're you holding up?"

She forced some lightness into her voice. "I'm okay.
Concentrating on things I can control, like earning money.
Earlier this week I called my old boss at Las Ventanas and

let him know I'm available for catering and special events. He brought me on as extra help for the re-launch gala next Friday."

As soon as she mentioned the resort, she wanted to bite her tongue. Chelsea had been the assistant manager of Las Ventanas until her boyfriend, Paul, got promoted to manager, cheated on her with the director of HR, and then dumped her at the holiday party after informing her he and Cindy were expecting a child. Chelsea had quit on the spot, and packed up for a fresh start, not to mention a better job, in Maui. But Cindy and Paul had hit the skids now, and they were managing to cause her grief from five thousand miles away. "If I see your ex or the skank he knocked up, I'll be sure to spill something on them."

Her best friend's laugh flooded the line, quickly covered by a cough. "Don't. You'll get in trouble, and I'll get a crazy phone call. Neither of us needs that."

"You're taking away all my fun," she complained, and fiddled with Booker's mug.

"There are better ways to have fun. Got any big plans tonight?"

"Actually, I've got this combo bachelor/bachelorette event—"

"Wow. You're working a lot, too."

"Not really. This is more like a—" Her thumb stilled midway along the mug handle as her eyes snagged on a small rectangular piece of paper on her counter. A check. From Booker. For three thousand dollars. A ball of ice landed hard in her stomach.

"More like a what?" Chelsea prompted.

A date? Uh-uh. It's a temp job, and you're 50 percent complete after tonight. Rehearsal dinner, wedding, reception, and then you're done. You've let this past week of sleepovers mess with your head. "No, you're right. It's a job." The laugh she mustered up sounded forced. "But it won't be too difficult," she finished lamely.

A few minutes later they said good-bye, but Laurie couldn't have repeated any portion of that conversation to save her life. She'd been too blindsided by the check to concentrate. Stupid. The money was part of their deal, and frankly, she needed it. Cindy would be in her face — and in the right — if she didn't get her deposit back on time.

But no amount of logic dislodged the cold weight in her gut. Instead it spread to her chest. She sank down to the kitchen floor and sat there, waiting for the pain to subside while a little voice in her head diagnosed the cause.

You haven't guarded your heart at all. You handed it to Booker a long time ago, and even when this arrangement ends, there's no getting it back.

Dammit, she really hated that little voice. Pressing her forehead to her knees, she drew in a deep breath. Her heart might choose to ignore reality, but her head couldn't. And her head was still in charge. This arrangement would come to an end — it had to, for both their sakes. She came with baggage she couldn't share. Not with anybody, and *especially* not with him.

. . .

Booker stretched his legs and tugged his tie off. The back compartment of the limousine looked a little worse for wear now that four other tipsy couples no longer shared the space. Empty glasses and crumpled cocktail napkins littered the consoles, along with a bunch of credit card receipts — wine clubs Kate had joined after a few too many tastings. Beside him, Lauralie looked into a compact mirror and applied lipstick with a little wand.

Watching her do it stirred up an urge to mess up all her

careful work. Slide his tongue between those plush, wet lips…
or his fingers…or whatever part of him she was game for, and
feel them close and swell around him.

"Did you have fun?" he asked, still watching her. She'd
gotten a little tipsy tonight, too, which wasn't like her. He
hadn't seen her drunk since she'd been sixteen. Yet despite
the extra cheer from the wine and the party, she seemed
subdued. Also not like her.

Blue eyes cut his way. She paused mid-swipe when she
caught him looking at her. "Yes."

"Nothing's wrong?"

She clicked the compact shut, screwed the wand back
into the thing, and dropped both into her small purse. Then
she turned to him. Her inspiring mouth stretched into a slow
smile—a slow, slightly off-center smile, completely at odds
with the smooth, sophisticated twist of her hair, her elegantly
bare shoulders, and the sleek white dress he'd longed to strip
off her the minute she'd walked down his stairs. "What could
be wrong?"

He reached over and ran his thumb over her chin. "You
tell me."

She lowered her eyelashes. The smile wavered for a
second, then recovered. "I might have had a little too much
fun." Her words didn't slur, but had the husky traces of a long
night.

Okay. She was tired. He punched the window down an
inch and breathed in the brisk, head-clearing air. Everything
he had in mind could wait until tomorrow morning. "I'll let
you in on a secret."

"What's your secret, Sheriff?" Oblivious to his
gentlemanly resolve, she snuggled into him and eased her feet
out of her sandals.

Thinking she was looking for a comfortable spot to relax
and close her eyes, he tucked her under his arm. The weight

of her breast pressed against his torso and teased him to a pleasant, semi-hard state. "Making sure you ladies had too much fun was the plan."

"I've never been wine tasting before." She tipped her head so her breath licked along the underside of his jaw. Her hand came to rest on his thigh, and his semi surged to something more urgent. "I didn't realize it was just a fancy way of getting loaded."

He dipped his chin to his chest to look at her. "Are you *loaded*?"

"I'm loose. The best man was loaded. That girl Mandy was loaded." Her smile widened. "Kate was *looooaded*."

He smiled, too, in part at her observation, and in part from the memory of Kate staggering into Aaron as they left the forth winery, looping her arms around his neck, and saying in a voice nowhere close to a whisper, *Hey, les elope. Ditch everyone and take the limo to Vegas, baby!*

"She attempted to drunk interrogate me twice tonight."

He tightened his arm and gave her a squeeze. "About what?"

"You. Us. Not in a mean way," she added, and then gave a dry laugh. "More like a 'Should I throw the bouquet your way?' way. I think we've got your family convinced we're a couple."

What would it take to convince *her*? "Are you basing that on tonight, or on the fact that my mom gave you a bag of sex toys?" Yeah, he'd gotten curious and peeked. And immediately wished he hadn't, but some things couldn't be unseen.

"That was unexpected, to say the least. Then again, I've never played the girlfriend role before. I wouldn't know what to expect."

"You're a natural." And he was stuck in a trap of his own making. He leaned his head back and stared at the leather-upholstered ceiling.

Her hand slid up his leg, and his hard-on throbbed. "You know what else I've never done?"

"Made a guy pass out from lack of blood flow to the brain?"

Her low laugh bounced her tits against his chest. Was she braless tonight?

She dropped her voice to a whisper even though the raised privacy panel ensured the driver couldn't overhear. "I've never done it in a limo. You?"

"Not since prom, Jailbait, but my house is all of five minutes away. We don't have time, unless you want to send this guy on a detour— Christ…" Her hand slipped inside the pocket of his pants, and he engaged the intercom.

"Yes, sir?" The driver's voice crackled from the front of the car.

"Nido Beach," he choked out as she traced his shaft through the lining of his pocket. Then she kneaded his balls. He caught her jaw in one hand and sank the other into the wild mane of curls she'd tamed and smoothed and pinned into submission. Everything gave under his touch. Her head tipped back. Her hair slid free of the pins. Her mouth opened generously for his tongue, and her scent wrecked his brain.

Her free hand trailed down the front of his shirt, until those agile fingers found his belt buckle and dispensed with it one-handed. Both hands came into play to unfasten his pants. The zipper rasped wickedly in the insulated luxury of the limousine.

Seconds later she had him out, jutting like a flagpole, her tight fist wrapped around the base of his cock and the untended inches pulsing in the cool, heavy air coming from the vents. She breathed into his ear, "I've never done this in a limo, either," and then scooted off the seat and settled onto her knees in front of him.

Her lips shined in the muted light. "Did you paint your lips for the occasion?"

One corner of her mouth lifted. "Maybe. Do you like the shade?" Then she lowered her head and kissed him, rubbing her lips over the tip. Pressure built fast, and terms like comfortable ceased to apply. A second later she eased back and admired the results. Sure enough, his crown sported a shimmer of red.

"Very pretty," he said through a tight throat.

She tipped her head to the side, in a show of diligent consideration. "It could use a little more color, down along here"—he groaned as her thumb traced a startlingly sensitive vein running the length of his shaft—"don't you think?"

"It's your project…fuuuuck." He caught a handful of the loose hair curtaining her face and twisted the strands around his fist so he could watch her take him deep. His fantasies of her soft, pink lips yielding to his cock paled in comparison to reality. He indulged them for as long as he could without endangering his ability to change her I Never status, but it didn't take long before the tight, hot haven at the back of her throat and the wet sounds of her working him wore away his reserves. He trapped her lithe body between his knees to keep her still, and, using her hair as a leash, slowly guided her mouth up his length. She kept the suction so tight the withdrawal drew his balls up, and popping himself free set off a blinding flash of light behind his eyes.

"Jailbait, next time we're in one of these I'm going to push your skirt up, part your legs, and give you a tongue lashing you'll never forget, but if you want to scratch 'Do it in a limo' off your I Never list tonight, you better get your ass on my lap right now."

She scrambled, he lifted, and a second later she straddled his hips. Her hands rested on his shoulders for balance. One hard tug pulled the top of her dress down to her ribs, revealing bare, pale skin and tight nipples.

He switched to an underhanded grip on her ass to try and maintain some control over the proceedings. "Put this"—he licked her straining nipple—"in my mouth."

A shiver cascaded down her spine. Eyes locked on his, she arched forward until her nipple grazed his lips. The barely there touch fluttered her eyelids. She tried to bear down and lower herself onto him, but he held her still. Once he was inside her, he had two, maybe three thrusts before he exploded. He had to find a way to take her with him. "In my mouth," he repeated, and leaned his head back against the seat to make her arch deeper. Helpful, because the position lifted her hips and left her more open for him. "I'm waiting."

"And you call *me* stubborn," she muttered, but complied. As she slowly fed her nipple between his lips, he fed his cock into her tight, wet channel.

"Ooooh." Her fingers threaded into his hair, and she pushed more of her breast into his mouth. He rewarded her with a hard suck and several more inches.

Her voice "That's…so…good. So good." He lowered her until she sat fully astride him, felt her quick inhale, and forced himself to give her a few seconds to get comfortable. She shifted her hips, dug her knees into the seat, and then exhaled a satisfied sigh. "Really, really good."

Hell yeah, it was good, but as soon as she squeezed those internal muscles, he knew he didn't have a chance in hell of taking her with him. He sealed his mouth around her other breast, lifted her a couple inches, and then brought her down solidly enough to make them both gasp. Another lift, another slam, another gasp, and he lost himself. He dragged her up and down his cock in fast, brutal bursts while he anchored her jiggling breast in his mouth and ravaged her nipple. And then he was coming. A blinding torrent of sensation that battered him, consumed him, ripped him away from her no matter how hard he tried to hold on.

The pain of her fingers twisting in his hair dragged him back, just in time to cover her mouth to stop the moans coming from her throat from escalating into cries that might reach their driver. He sucked her breast, shoved two fingers between her lips, and flexed every muscle he had between his navel and his knees to send her over.

She went. Rising up. Crashing down. Shuddering against him while she sucked his fingers and hugged his shaft. Finally, she bowed back, palms planted on his knees, center dragging over his abs, and jerked once, twice, before falling forward and collapsing over him.

Her arms circled his shoulders. Her cheek rested on the top of his head. "Holy shit," he murmured against her breast. "I stand corrected. I never did it in a limo until tonight. Not properly."

She laughed. "I'm no expert, but I'd say we did it proper tonight…uh-oh. We're stopping."

Sure enough, the limo rolled to a halt. Then the driver's voice invaded their space. "Nido Beach, sir."

His fingers hovered over the intercom, but before he could respond, she hitched her top up, slipped off his lap, and pushed her skirt down. "I'm going for a swim."

"What?" Maybe she was wasted after all. Water temps were sixty degrees, max, this time of year, but before he could remind her she bounded out the door. A blast of cool air washed over his wrung-out dick before he tucked it into his pants and dragged his zipper up. He burned through another minute shucking off his shoes and socks, and then chased after her. The sliver of moon barely lit her as she raced across the sand and into the water, long hair flying behind her like a banner for him to capture.

Foamy waves crashed around his calves before he closed in on her. His heart pounded, a little from the sprint, but mainly because she stood there like a mirage of moonlight and the tide. Fascinating, but fundamentally elusive.

That's exactly what she is.

He immediately rejected the thought. She was no mirage, and neither was the connection between them. She could run all night if she wanted, but she wouldn't outrun it. Maybe she realized as much, because she looked over her shoulder and her eyes locked on him. The remnants of her smile faded.

"What's wrong?"

"Nothing. Everything's good. We're halfway done." Her big-eyed gaze drifted away, and she chewed her thumbnail.

Something definitely worried her. Money? "Did you get the check I left?"

Her chin came up. "Yes." The smile returned, but not quite the free and easy one from a moment ago. "Thanks."

He took a step closer, grappling with the uncomfortable feeling he'd asked the wrong question. "You're welcome. Anything else on your mind?"

"Just this." Her smile turned innocent an instant before she flicked her foot across the surface of the water, splashing him.

Yeah, he'd definitely fucked that up, somehow. Now he could either be an asshole and hammer at her—which would only make her less likely to talk—or let it go for now. He let it go. "Jailbait, don't make me haul you off this beach a second time." A bigger wave rolled in, pushing her toward him. He took her hand, and then moved their joined hands to the small of her back. Her palm settled against the front of his shirt.

"On what grounds, Sheriff? I don't have a curfew anymore."

"I'm imposing one. No swimming after dusk."

"Ha. How do you plan to enforce this new curfew?"

He lowered his head and kissed her. Cool, salty lips parted

for him, but instead of claiming what she offered, he rubbed his lips over hers, warming them, before catching her lower lip between his teeth and licking the salt from her skin. Slowly he drew back, his teeth lightly tugging and scraping the tender flesh trapped between. When it sprang free, her sigh fluttered away on the breeze.

She blinked her eyes open and gave him another strangely sad smile. "If that's your idea of a deterrent, I should warn you, you're going to have people breaking curfew left and right." Slow, bluesy notes from an acoustic guitar drifted toward them from somewhere down the beach. Her brow lifted. "There's one now."

A flex of his arm pulled her closer. He wrapped his other arm around her waist, and swayed her gently in time with the music. "This particular curfew applies only to women who have their way with me in a limo."

"All right then, I'm busted. Do what you've gotta do." But she leaned into him, and she matched her steps to his. In the distance, a soulful voice joined the serenade, layering on moody lyrics about love with a stranger—the stranger the better.

The moment stretched as they swayed to the music and the rhythm of the waves. Eventually she sighed and looked up at the star-strewn sky. He thought she might start the conversation again, and tell him whatever she'd been about to say before he'd jumped the gun. Instead she whispered, "Jesus, four wineries, and my head's a mess. We should go. All this romance is wasted on us, Booker."

His head was suddenly, perfectly clear. She needed the romance, even if she claimed otherwise. And he needed to give it to her, because the bond between them was more than just some undefined connection. It had a name. Sometime between dragging a headstrong teen off this very beach and slow dancing in ankle-deep surf with the beautiful, complicated woman she'd become, he'd fallen in love.

And you can't say shit to her about it.

"Speak for yourself, Jailbait. I happen to appreciate dancing by starlight every once in awhile."

"Play that card at the right time, I'll bet it someday wins you the woman of your dreams."

He hoped. Ten plus years in law enforcement had taught him how to bide his time and manipulate a situation to his advantage, but when given the choice he preferred a straightforward approach. Lauralie, and circumstances, hadn't given him that choice, and now the scheme he'd manipulated her into for the sake of helping her prevented him from telling her how he felt. If *she* said the words first, that would be different, but hell had a better chance of freezing over before Lauralie Peterson left herself emotionally vulnerable to anyone.

Which put it back on him. He understood her well enough to know he meant more to her than she wanted to admit. This was no longer a sport to her. Even so, throwing down an "I love you," pushed the boundaries of fair play. Love wasn't part of their deal. If he added it in now, he was unilaterally changing the rules on her while there was money at stake. Money she was counting on. No matter how much a part of him shouted *Fuck fairness*, he couldn't do it. Not when waiting a few weeks would level their playing field.

But he could and would keep the game tight. Keep the pressure on. The lights from Las Ventanas twinkled on the bluff like a reminder. "I spoke to my mom today."

"How's mom?" She drew back a little, despite her casual response.

"Ambitious." He kept his hands at her waist and continued their unhurried two-step. "She called to inform me I'm expected to attend the Las Ventanas re-launch party. Apparently she's got her eye on a business relationship with the St. Sebastian family. I think she'd like to see Best Life products in all the guestrooms. Want to be my date?"

Her steps faltered. "I can't. I'm already going."

He stopped, and told himself to remain calm. "With who?"

"With the hired help. I'll be there as a server. My old boss put out a call for extra hands—at a really good rate, I might add—and I answered."

"Cancel. I've got you covered." The words were out before he realized how they sounded. Okay, *that* was why any discussion of their feelings needed to wait until after the wedding.

"I can't." She backed away and wrapped her arms around herself. "I can't afford to piss off one of my best sources for catering jobs with a last minute cancellation. I need real work. What if Chelsea's bonus falls through? What if the insurance company finds some loophole to justify not paying?"

Then he'd figure out some other way to help her. But he couldn't tell her that either, and what came out instead was a highly frustrated, "Fine. Forget I asked."

"Thanks for understanding." She started toward the limo. He bit back a curse, because he knew damn well he'd just convinced her he didn't understand.

Chapter Thirteen

The St. Sebastian family knew how to throw a party, Laurie decided as she carried a tray of cannoli-cream-filled chocolate cups toward the dessert buffet, navigating a crowd of people in evening clothes that cost more than her rent. Not that it took a genius to master the formula. Throw open the doors of a beautiful, landmark hotel after giving it a multimillion dollar facelift, invite the right mix of local luminaries, celebrities and media personalities, and pour liberal amounts of top-shelf champagne over everything.

Around her, those lucky enough to make the guest list talked, laughed, and posed for pictures destined for the pages of aspirational magazines. Readers with disposable income would soak in the glossy images and immediately realize Las Ventanas was *the* destination for the hip and glamorous.

Attending the festivities as one of the extra hands they'd recruited to help with the party took most of the glamour out of the night for her, but a girl had to do what a girl had to do. Earlier today she'd paid bills and mailed out refund checks to half the clients she owed. She was tapped out, and being

Booker's date-for-hire was no kind of long-range solution. Getting back on the roster of extras Las Ventanas called on to handle large events was.

Three years spent as a pastry chef at the resort meant she knew the kitchen, most of the staff, and enjoyed a little more respect than the average temp. But a part of her less receptive to logic couldn't help feeling like she'd taken a giant step backward. Back to a kitchen that wasn't hers, and recipes she'd had no input on, following someone else's directions. Hearing the sous chef call, "Peterson, you know the difference between vanilla zabaglione and white-chocolate mousse. Get out there and tell me what we're running low on," had only underscored the fact.

Getting "out there" meant a chance to escape the kitchen for a moment, and the nagging fear this whole working-for-someone-else situation might be more than a temporary thing. She had a job to do—as quickly and invisibly as possible, but she found herself dawdling. Booker circulated somewhere in the crowd and she wanted to see him.

Unfortunately, milling bodies prevented her from getting a good view the room.

And you're not here to take in the scene. Stay on task.

Right. She concentrated on unloading her tray of cannoli onto the buffet and noting which items they needed to replenish next. When she finished, she straightened, and inadvertently bumped someone standing behind her.

Apology at the ready, she turned, but it stuck in her throat when she found herself face-to-face with Miranda McQueen. *Fucking awesome.* She swallowed and forced the words out. "Sorry, ma'am."

Miranda's dismissive gaze raked over her white smock, and for a second, Laurie thought the woman might not recognize her. No such luck. Those pale, icicle eyes narrowed as they studied her face, and then came the frown.

"You."

"Laurie," she supplied.

"Of course. Booker's interesting friend." One corner of her mouth tightened into her haughty version of a smirk. "Not on the guest list tonight?"

Laurie straightened, uncomfortably aware of the satisfaction Miranda took from the discrepancy in their positions. She refused to give the old stick the added satisfaction of seeing her sweat the situation. "What can I tell you, Miranda? I'm a woman of many talents."

"I'll bet you are, although…" Miranda's gaze shifted to somewhere over Laurie's shoulder, and her smirk stretched into a serpentine smile. "Perhaps not quite as interesting and talented as you like to think."

Laurie turned. Groups of people separated at that moment, and left her with a sightline to the edge of the terrace. Booker stood there, effortlessly handsome in his tuxedo, completely at ease in the lavish surroundings. And why wouldn't he be? Even if his position as sheriff didn't earn him a spot on the guest list for events like this, his last name did. Hell, he grew up in this world. He knew it well. He *belonged*.

The thoughts registered along with a realization he was deep in conversation—eye-to-eye, nothing else exists conversation—with a slim, raven-haired beauty who hung on his every word. They leaned toward each other as they spoke. Her hand rested on his forearm.

Something hot and volatile boiled through her blood, leaving her shaky and short of breath. Her fingernails dug into her palms as she fought an urge to stride over and knock the woman's hand away.

Cause a scene, look like a crazy freak—make Denise proud.

"It appears Booker has other interests, doesn't it? Do you recognize her?" Miranda's insidious questions pricked like needles. "Arden St. Sebastian," she said when Laurie didn't reply, "of St. Sebastian Luxury Resorts. A lovely girl from an excellent family. I'm a wedding planner, not a matchmaker, but I have to admit they look good together. She and Booker have quite a bit in common."

Booker leaned closer to the woman, practically whispering in her ear.

"I'm sure," she managed through a throat clenched as tight as her fists. The overly familiar hand on his arm didn't belong to just any woman. It belonged to a beautiful, privileged hotel heiress. *Belonged.* There was that word again. Miranda McQueen belonged. Ethan Booker belonged. Arden St. Sebastian most definitely belonged. The only person in the room right now who didn't belong?

Lauralie Peterson.

She should fix that before she did something stupid. With the tray tucked under her arm, she stepped away. "Nice bumping into you"—*Lauralie Peterson, master of sarcasm*—"I have to get back to work."

• • •

Numbers told a story, even when they didn't add up. The number of times he'd texted Lauralie during the party, hoping to spend a few minutes with her during a break? Three. The number of times she'd replied? Zero.

Fair enough. She'd been working, but more numbers factored in, such as the 1:45 a.m. staring back at Booker from the screen of his phone, and the three additional unanswered texts he'd sent since leaving Las Ventanas. The story these numbers told didn't make a fuckload of scnsc yct, but he intended to get some clarity right now.

He exited his car and took the walkway leading to her door, equal parts relieved and annoyed to see light shining from her windows. He deliberately slowed his steps, letting the relief sink in—his line of work left nasty possibilities in his head when someone suddenly went incommunicado—but as the knowledge she wasn't lying in a ditch somewhere eased the knot of tension in his gut, it fired up the itch of irritation under his skin. Despite three straight weeks of spending nights together, despite knowing damn well he expected to hear from her, and despite his texts, she'd gone home after the party without so much as a word of explanation. She owed him one, and he wasn't leaving until he had it.

After a warning knock, he turned the knob and pushed the door open. The scent of fresh-baked…something…hit him first, and pulled his attention across the living room to the kitchen beyond. She stood there, framed by the pass-through, wearing a white apron, and holding a chocolate-covered spatula midair.

He stepped inside and shut the door behind him. "You should lock your door."

She dropped the spatula into the mixing bowl that sat on the counter in front of her and then wiped her hands on a towel before fixing the sliding strap of the little black slip she had on beneath the apron. "You should wait 'til you're invited in."

Those flashing blue eyes were all it took to have his dick lifting. "The evidence suggests I would have been waiting all night." He crossed the room until he stood on the other side of the counter. "Apparently sometime during the last few hours you lost the ability to communicate."

"Maybe you were too busy communicating with someone else tonight to notice me making an attempt?"

The moody comment surprised him. Her, too, judging by how she snapped her mouth shut, and began rearranging ingredients on the counter.

"Care to elaborate, Jailbait? Right now I have no idea

what you're talking about."

"You know what? I don't care to." She picked up the mixing bowl and began stirring the contents with the spatula. "I'm tired."

The vigorous stirring jiggled her tits. If she kept that up, this was going to be a short conversation. "That's why you're baking up a storm in the middle of the night?"

"Baking relaxes me. Unlike uninvited company and unwanted conversation. If you feel like *communicating*, go find Arden St. Sebastian. I'm sure she'd be more than happy to continue whatever fascinating discussion you were having tonight while eye fucking each other in the middle of a goddamn party."

Okay, yes, he had talked with Arden tonight, one-on-one and at some length, but there'd been absolutely no eye fucking on either of their parts. Obviously, Lauralie had seen them and jumped to a different conclusion. Her misread of the situation was clearly pissing the shit out of her, and while he never would have intentionally toyed with her emotions, the jealousy brought an almost obscene level of gratification. A laugh escaped before he could hold it back.

Her head jerked up and she glared at him while she continued stirring her frosting with real violence now. "Get out."

Well aware he risked bodily harm, he rounded the counter and strode into her kitchen. She'd been busy. Flour covered the surface of the butcher-block island, and a rack of pastries sat cooling on the counter. "Not on your life "

She slammed the bowl onto the counter and turned on him. "Was it her?"

"I don't know what you're asking."

Her barefoot strides closed the distance between them and she stabbed her finger into his chest. Her fingertip left a white imprint on his tuxedo jacket. "You do so. Was she your first choice? Is she the reason you came sniffing around my door on New Year's Eve, desperate for a rebound fuck?"

He would have laughed again at the absurdity of the notion he'd had any agenda except being with her when he'd shown up at her apartment that night, but she seemed to genuinely believe he might. "Jailbait, I barely know her."

"Yeah. Right. You always find a quiet corner in the middle of a party to have an intimate chat with some girl you barely know?" She punctuated the accusation with another poke. "Do you have any idea what kind of an idiot I felt like, standing there while Miranda McQueen went on about what a lovely couple you two make? I—I don't need this. And based on what everybody saw tonight, neither do you." Another poke. "The deal's off."

His patience ran out. He grabbed her wrist and stepped forward, forcing her to step back.

"Hey…" She tugged her wrist but he didn't let go.

"This isn't about our deal."

Her laugh held no humor. "Only someone with money would say that."

"Bullshit." He took another step forward. "It's *never* been about the money, and we both know it. Let's move that out of our way right now." He let go of her and dug a check out of his wallet. A rummage through her junk drawer yielded a pen. He scrawled out a check for three grand and held it out to her. "Invest it in your business, spend it on therapy, or bury it in the sand, right next to your head. I don't care what you do with it, but money's not between us anymore."

She backed up a step and glared at him. "*I* don't need therapy—"

"You do, if you honestly think there's room in *my* head for anyone but you." He cornered her between his body and the kitchen island, and shoved the check into the pocket of her apron. "Do you?" He flattened his palms on the butcher block on either side of her and waited for an answer.

She tossed her head back, but kept her lips stubbornly closed.

"You think when I'm here"—he reached under the apron, under her slip, and cupped her—"I'm fantasizing about anyone else?"

Her eyelids lowered a notch and color whipped into her cheeks. "I don't care."

He curled his other arm around her waist and lifted her onto the island. The landing sent up a cloud of flour. The rolling pin she'd left there tumbled to the floor with a solid *thud*. "You're so jealous, you can't think straight—"

"I'm not jealous." She stressed this with a roll of her hips. "I *never* get jealous."

She did get turned on, though. Her warm, soft flesh kissed his palm. He eased his fingers inside her. Slim thighs clamped his hips. "You are. You know why?"

"Stop talking." She tore at his fly. He kept up the slow, shallow strokes while she freed him from his pants. A second later he nudged the head of his cock down her center. She fell back onto her elbows.

"Do you know why?" he repeated, and retraced the path. She refused to answer, but her legs fluttered impatiently.

He surged into her, deep enough to bow her spine and send her head tipping back. Her knees lifted. He hitched them into the crooks of his arms and pulled her toward him. More flour filled the air. "Because you're not pretending anymore. This is real."

She whipped her head back and forth. "No."

He withdrew and thrust again. "This thing between us is real."

Her fingers dug into his scalp and she drew his head down to hers. "I don't get involved..."

"Until me." He drove into her again.

She gasped. Inner muscles fluttered around him. "No."

Flour stung his eyes. He ran his mouth along the side of her throat and tasted it on her skin. "You want this to be real." He risked another thrust, even as he felt his balls draw up and a familiar heat flow down his spine.

"You're wrong." The words were a desperate whisper. She reared up, so suddenly their foreheads would have collided if he hadn't straightened. White flecks danced in the air between them. "Right here, right now. This is as real as it gets." She squeezed her eyes shut and shuddered.

One semi-sane part of his mind told him to stop trying to bully her into admitting her feelings. It wasn't the right approach. But he couldn't stop. Screw patience. Screw fairness. He was in love with her, dammit, and he needed at least this much in return or he was letting her limit them to sex. This was going to hurt like a motherfucker, but he couldn't settle for just sex. He pulled out.

"Booker!" Her eyes flew open, and she grabbed onto his shoulders. "Don't."

He shook his head. "Right here, right now, isn't enough. Not anymore. You have to do better." Need closed in on him like a predator, mocking his threat.

"I can't. I—" Her voice cracked, and then, thank Christ, her resolve. "Oh, God. I want this to be real." A tear leaked from the corner of her eye and ran down her cheek, leaving a wet trail in the flour dusting her skin.

He caught it with his lips. "I know. I know. Don't cry."

"I can't help it." She pressed her face against his neck. "I'm terrified."

"You don't have anything to be afraid of. I'm going to make you feel so good." He pushed back inside her and they both groaned. "So fucking good."

Burying his fingers in her hair, he drew her head back until her watery gaze met his. Then he plunged deep.

She cried out at the impact. More tears rolled down her cheeks.

"Is that good, Lauralie?"

"Yes." She nodded. Wide, dark pupils focused on him.

He rocked into her again, and again. She matched the pace, bracing her weight on her hands and surging to meet him. Holding there longer as the intensity mounted. "You know why it's so good?"

"I don't know. I don't…know." On the last, gasping word her body pulled tight. She threw back her head and cried out as the tension dissolved into long, helpless shudders.

Before the sheer power of it sucked him in, too, he managed to say, "Because this is real."

Chapter Fourteen

Laurie let her arms flop to either side of her head, and opened one eye. Her view consisted of the old, fluorescent tube lights in her ceiling. She stared at them through a fog of sweat, tears, and flour. Her words, Booker's words—the whole tangled mess—echoed around her in her head. Which scared her more, the words or the man who wrung them out of her?

Hard to say. The man had her pinned under him, his heart asserting its slow, steady rhythm on hers. Big hands cupped her ass and her legs dangled over his arms.

This is bad. The thought rushed into her mind, triggered a surge of adrenalin that made her muscles jump. A flight instinct. *You're in over your head.*

"Stop panicking, Jailbait." Booker straightened and looked down at her. Flour lightened his eyelashes and brows. For some crazy reason she found it endearing. "You're fine. We were overdue for this conversation. Now that we've had it, you can calm down."

She propped herself up on one arm. Panic gave way to something else. He'd manipulated her. "Don't tell me to calm down. You deliberately made me jealous—"

"No." He shook his head. "You did that all on your own."

"Really? You wouldn't have thought anything of it if I'd been the one snuggled into a corner tonight, whispering in someone else's ear."

He chewed on that for a moment, and then inclined his head. "Arden's dealing with unwanted attention from an as yet unidentified person, or persons. She asked me about our progress with the investigation. That's what we discussed."

Shit. The scene replayed in her mind, with the distortion of her overheated emotions removed. Details took on a new cast. Arden's unsmiling expression hadn't been seductive, but anxious. She'd held onto to his arm out of a need for reassurance. "I didn't realize…" She felt like an ass.

"It's not public information." He smoothed his thumb over her cheekbone. "For various reasons, we want to keep it that way. Tonight's party wasn't the right time or place to discuss the matter. I hadn't planned to. I'm sure she didn't either, because generally, she views the whole thing as a nuisance, but I think the crowd made her uneasy."

"Understandable." But dammit, a lack of justifiable outrage left her defenseless. "Forget I said anything. In fact"—she tried to slide away and get to her feet—"forget everything I said."

He didn't move. "Not a chance. You said it. I heard it. We move forward from here. Try to be a little brave."

She shoved at him, harder, because the walls were closing in. The air itself threatened to crush her. She could stuff her own feelings into a box and lock them away where they couldn't do any damage—hardly any. She'd practiced the skill her entire life. But this? Nothing had prepared her for this.

"Booker"—she gestured between them—"this is a bad bet. *I'm* a bad bet." The words spilled out fast, with a manic edge that was pure Denise. The risks felt too close. *He* felt too close, but for whatever reason, her hands didn't get the memo she was pushing him away. Her fingers curled around the lapels of his tux and held on. "My life is completely fucked up. Every part of it—you don't even know—and, yes, I'm scared the mess will splatter onto you, and I'm going to fuck you up, too…"

His mouth closed over hers. His tongue swept aside the warnings she wanted to give him. When he drew back, he framed her face in his hands and waited until she looked him square in the eye. "I'm not so easy to fuck up. Trust me."

He didn't pose it as a question. He expected her trust, end of story. And she did trust him. *But there are things you haven't told him, and the moment to speak up came and went a long time ago. If he ever finds out, he'll see it as a betrayal.* She let out a breath and sagged against him. "Booker, it's not you. It's me I don't trust."

"Work on that." He lifted her off the island. "This is real, and I'm not going to let you fuck it up."

• • •

"Hey, Babycakes, my bonus is back on track."

"Woo-hoo!" For once, Laurie didn't try to temper her enthusiasm. She switched her phone to her other ear and took the withdrawal receipt the ATM spit at her, ignoring the anemic account balance listed there. The bonus was good news. Why not have a little faith in the powers of good, and embrace it?

"Better still, I'll be in Montenido day after tomorrow," Chelsea added.

"You're right. That is even better." She walked down Ocean Avenue, away from the bank, slowing her steps as she passed an empty storefront with a FOR LEASE sign in the window. "When do you arrive? We need to celebrate."

High rent district, she warned herself, but still ended

up peering through the glass. It couldn't hurt to look. If her insurance company paid out, plus Chelsea's bonus...

Her imagination immediately filled the shop with an order counter and a couple display cases while her best friend ran through her itinerary. Chelsea's flight arrived tomorrow night, but she had work-related plans that evening. Not a problem, because Laurie had Kate and Aaron's rehearsal dinner. As they talked through the logistics, it hit her how much their lives had changed since they'd last seen each other. Chelsea Wayne, people-pleaser and queen of leading with her heart, was neck deep in a no-strings fling with Rafe St. Sebastian, while Laurie Peterson, the queen of guarding her heart, was in an honest-to-god relationship. Granted, the more she listened, the more Chelsea and Rafe's no-strings arrangement showed signs of at least a few tethers, but Chelsea wasn't ready to hear it.

Laurie sympathized. Chelsea's ex had bruised her heart, and protecting herself from another battering was a normal response. Laurie's heart had been bruised at birth—probably earlier—which might explain why it had taken losing the thing she cherished most to finally force her to lower the shields and reach out. Maybe the universe had been trying to teach her an important lesson? Namely, she wasn't alone. When she'd needed help, people had come forward. Chelsea, with the bonus. Her friends at Las Ventanas, with the extra work.

Booker.

She'd definitely lowered her shields where he was concerned, let her heart lead, and inconceivably, she hadn't fucked things up.

Yet, the voice in her head—the one that sounded like Denise—insisted on adding.

She shushed it. Yes, there were things she hadn't told him, but she was starting to believe that everything would work out, even if she kept a few sketchy details to herself. According to the insurance adjuster, the check was all but in the mail. They only awaited the investigator's final report in order to pay her claim.

Chelsea signed off with a promise to meet up the day after tomorrow—Valentine's Day—and check out the potential new location for Babycakes.

Babycakes by the Beach. She liked the sound of that.

So stop expecting everything to turn to shit.

Determined to follow her own advice, she took down the realtor's name and number from the For Lease sign. Her phone rang as she was inputting the contact information. She hit connect and brought it to her ear. Either her scrupulously organized friend had forgotten some detail, or she was ready to talk about the situation with Rafe. "Miss me already?"

"I always miss my baby girl."

Denise's voice sent an invisible army of ants over her skin. "What do you want?" She glanced around, half expecting to see her mother standing across the street, watching her. The empty sidewalk did nothing to alleviate her dread.

"I want to talk to you, sweetheart. I heard about your poor little bakery. I want to help."

"Thanks, but I don't need your help." She turned on her heel and walked fast toward her car.

"Oh, I think you do."

The snide note stopped Laurie in her tracks. "Whatever you *think* you know, you're wrong."

"I know I got a message from an insurance investigator, who has some questions for me. I'm wondering if he's aware you were in the bakery the morning of the fire, or that you emptied the safe."

The ants swarmed up her neck, leaving the rest of her icy cold. "It's irrelevant." She spoke slowly, calmly. "I didn't set the fire."

"Of course you didn't. But those pieces of information… they complicate things, don't they? I bet your insurance company would find those facts very problematic."

A coppery taste in her mouth made her realize she'd bitten her cuticle. She made herself stop and take a deep breath. "I have absolutely no motive for torching my business. Anyone investigating me will see that. I wasn't losing money and I didn't have a need for fast cash—"

"Your dear mother's got a great deal of need. Medical expenses, and whatnot. My situation's desperate and a devoted daughter might do something drastic to help."

"I'm not a devoted daughter, and anyone who knows me will testify to that."

"Testify? Sweet, naive Lauralie, they don't need to accuse you of arson. A friend of mine told me there's a tiny little clause in most insurance contracts that says you'll give them complete cooperation when they investigate your claim. If you don't, they can deny it. Now, I'm no lawyer, but lying doesn't sound very cooperative to me. How will it sound to them, do you think?"

Not good. "I didn't lie." She hurried to her car, got in, and slammed the door. "I answered all their questions."

"You left something out."

Her conscience said the same thing. A lie by omission still amounted to a lie. But she refused to admit as much to Denise. "You've got ten seconds to tell me what you want or I'm hanging up." A fist squeezed her middle, causing waves of nausea.

"Half."

The fist closed tighter, making it hard to breathe. "Half of *what*?"

"Half the money, baby girl. You pay me my half and I'll keep those little details to myself. Otherwise, I have to pick up the phone and tell that nice man from the insurance company the whole truth."

"Truth…" The single word practically strangled her.

Truth? She never should have given in to her mother's threats in the first place. Another truth? If she caved again now she'd always be hostage to Denise's demands. She'd pay, and pay, and pay, both in the form of money and self-respect.

More truth? She *had* been in the bakery that morning, she *had* emptied the safe, and those messy facts didn't change the essential truth—she didn't have a freaking clue how the fire started. It was exactly the kind of random disaster for which she carried insurance. But in a moment of weakness, she'd screwed herself, and if she ever wanted to face her reflection again without flinching, she had to draw the line. Yes, she risked having her claim denied, and the domino effect looked a lot like defaulting on her loan, declaring bankruptcy, and spending years wage-slaving her ass off to get her head above water again.

Demoralizing as those realizations were, they didn't account for the sour panic rising in the back of her throat. No matter what move she made at this point, she risked losing Booker's trust. She'd kept secrets from him, and if he found out, he might never forgive her. He'd sworn he wouldn't let her fuck them up, but she'd fucked them up before they'd gotten started…

"Do we have a deal?" The impatience in Denise's voice sounded like fingernails tapping a table.

Jesus, she was going to be sick. "No."

"Don't tell me no. You think I won't—"

She disconnected the call, and then fumbled to block the number. Once she accomplished that, she rested her forehead against the steering wheel and closed her eyes. Rapid, unsteady breaths filled the car. Hers. When they leveled off a little, she lifted her head, and tapped her phone to bring up her call log. The insurance adjuster's number sat near the top of the list. She hit it, and waited as the line rang.

Things had officially turned to shit.

Chapter Fifteen

Laurie finished blow-drying her hair into loose waves, and stared at her reflection. Two days of hearing nothing from the insurance adjuster after sending him her updated statement had left shadows under her eyes, but makeup masked the worst of it. Resolving to come clean to Booker might have helped, too, although her stomach twisted just thinking about the conversation. She expected him any minute, and promised herself she'd tell him as soon as he walked in the door.

Lipstick in hand, she strode from the bathroom to the bedroom. The small, silk purse she'd chosen for tonight sat on her dresser. Hopefully Best Life had no issues with the silkworm. She opened the bag and tucked the lipstick in the inside pocket, next to her phone, noticing a waiting message in the process. A screen swipe later Booker's voice came over the line.

I'm leaving the station now. Going to be about ten minutes late, but I'll make it up to you. I've got some news you'll appreciate.

Yeah, she had some news for him, too, but nothing he'd appreciate. And nothing she wanted to bring up over the phone or in a rushed conversation on the way to a family event. Maybe him running late worked out for the best? She'd wait until after the rehearsal dinner to tell him about... everything.

She texted him a reply.

Save yourself ten minutes. I'll meet you there. I have something to tell you, too. Can we talk after dinner?

A moment later an income text arrived.

I have plans for your mouth tonight, but I'm sure we can squeeze in a conversation.

The only thing she envisioned him doing after their conversation was washing his hands of her, and she vowed she'd make it easy for him—he was entitled to take the high road right out of her life, and no matter how much it hurt to let him go, she would. Strong, trustworthy, intrinsically *good* Booker deserved someone equally strong. Equally trustworthy.

Since the night of the Las Ventanas party, she'd fooled herself into thinking she could be that woman, but true to the woman she actually was, she'd gambled with fate rather than face the consequences of her bad decisions.

Taking the gamble only underscored her lack of strength and integrity, and losing promised to cost more than she'd realized she'd put at risk, but if she truly cared about Booker the one thing she could do at this point was help cut *his* losses.

Start by being on time tonight. She dropped her phone into her purse, grabbed her keys, and headed out, only to skid to a halt as she approached her carport. The back end of the Expedition tilted noticeably to the right, thanks to a tire flat.

Shit. She kicked off her heels, and stowed them, plus her purse, in the car. Twenty minutes and several curse words later she raced back inside her apartment to clean up, and then rushed back to the car. She was going to be late.

One the way to Las Ventanas she considered and rejected ways to explain things to Booker. Should she start with her mother's call and the demand for half the insurance payout in exchange for silence? No, that would mean backtracking to the real issue—the one she felt most guilty about—not admitting up front she'd been in the bakery the morning of the fire, paying her mother to leave her alone.

This isn't a donut, Peterson. You can't sugarcoat it.

Lead with the first bad decision and go from there, she decided as she weaved her way through Las Ventanas' lobby to Ventanas del Mar, the five-star restaurant where Booker, his family, and the other members of the wedding party occupied a private table on the terrace.

Booker spotted her first and stood. His dark eyes scanned her face as she neared, and she did her best to look normal. He stepped forward and kissed her cheek. "Is everything okay?"

"I'm fine." To the table, she added, "Sorry I'm late."

"You're just in time," Kate called from her spot mid-table as a waiter arrived with a tray of glasses. "We ordered champagne."

Booker guided her to the empty chair next to his and held it for her. Before he stepped away, he paused and leaned close to her ear. "What's wrong?"

"I had a flat," she said, and offered him what she hoped passed for a smile while he took his seat. Aaron passed her a flute of champagne, and she transferred the smile to him, but it died on her lips when a skinny, red-haired woman in tight jeans and an even tighter sweater staggered through the French doors, with the silver-haired maître d' in hot pursuit.

Fuck, no. She wanted to stand, but her body refused to

move.

"Madam, please." The maître d' made a grab for Denise's arm.

"Get the *hell* away from me," she slurred, and shoved the dark-suited man in the shoulder with one hand. The other clutched a half-empty liter of gin.

"Security is on the way," he murmured.

The discretion was wasted. Everyone in the vicinity turned to stare. Everyone. Belligerent drunk women cursing out the staff weren't the norm at Las Ventanas.

"There she is." Denise elbowed the maître d' away from her. "I told you my daughter's here. And there she is." She pointed at Laurie and grinned.

Booker got to his feet. His movement freed her from the paralysis of mortification. Her legs finally responded to the urgent signals her brain sent and she surged out of her chair. "What are you doing here?"

"Looking for you, Lauralie. Our last conversation ended so abruptly, and then you didn't return my calls, so you left me no choice. I drove all the way to this Godforsaken town to talk some sense into you. I turned onto your street in time to see that big, shiny SUV of yours pull out. It's so easy to follow, I just tagged along." She stopped, tipped the bottle, and took a long drink. "And now it all makes sense."

"Let's take this outside, Mom." Funny, how calm she sounded. Nobody would guess her pulse raced so fast her head felt light.

"Sit," Booker said to her. "I'll handle this."

Okay, maybe someone might guess, but she couldn't sit, because this was beyond handling. She took a step toward her mother. Denise circled to the other side of the table and kept on talking.

"Now I know why you don't give a shit about the insurance money. Who cares if they know you were in the bakery that morning, emptying your safe? Who cares if they deny your claim? You've got a bigger payday lined up."

"You're wrong," Laurie shot back, but her voice now held a fast, desperate edge. Her legs started to shake.

Denise laughed and crossed her arms, letting the bottle dangle from her fingers. "Don't tell me I'm wrong. You're sitting with Rebecca Motherfucking Booker, all tight with her son. You're trying to cut me out, little girl, but you cut me, and I cut back. I offered you a fair deal. I'd keep quiet about a few inconvenient facts you preferred the insurance company never know, and all I requested in return was half the money. But you're selfish. You think you're so much better than me. Always have. Well guess what, Lauralie, we're exactly the same, and I'm going to make sure everybody knows it."

She felt rather than saw everyone at the table shift their attention to her, and her cheeks burned. Booker reached Denise and took her arm. She tried to jerk away and fumbled the bottle. It crashed to the terrace and shattered.

"Godammit! Look what you made me do."

Laurie stepped over the glass to Denise's other side. "Booker, please." She couldn't meet his eyes. "Go back to your family. This is my mess to deal with."

He wasn't a man who lost his temper often, but the grim look he sent her told her he barely had a lock on it now. "This is *not* your mess to deal with. It never should have been, but it sure as hell isn't anymore, and I thought we were clear on that. Apparently I was wrong."

"Booker—"

"Sit down, Lauralie, or I'll charge you with obstruction." He hauled Denise around and marched her toward the terrace doors just as two members of hotel security and two deputies arrived.

"Am I under arrest?" Denise slurred.

"Hell yes," Booker answered.

She burst into loud, dramatic sobs.

Cut, print, wrap. Scene complete. Numbness settled over her as she watched Booker hand Denise off to a young deputy. The poor kid's expression said he'd rather touch a live rattler than touch the drunk-assed, bitch-load of crazy that was her mother, but he steered her toward the exit.

Booker spared a backward glance at the group. "Kate, Aaron, congratulations—"

"Booker, wait…" She took a hesitant step toward him, but he shook his head, turned away, and followed the deputies.

She turned to find the entire table staring at her, silent and shocked. Hot, sharp shame split the cocoon of numbness holding her together.

Get out of here. Now.

"I—I'm sorry," she offered, and managed to propel herself forward despite her unsteady legs. "I should go." Her purse dangled from the back of her chair—the satin bag she'd deliberately chosen so as not to offend Booker's mom.

Good news. Your purse didn't offend anyone.

She snatched it up and hurried toward the doors. Behind her, a voice called, "Laurie…"

Booker's mom. She quickened her pace. By the time she reached the lobby she was running, heels skidding on the marble. The voice in her head kept repeating the same thing. *Go. Go. Go.*

She went, as fast as physics and speed limits allowed— almost crashing into a line of garbage bins as she took the turn into her complex—but not stopping until she closed her apartment door behind her. Then came the crash. Her, to the floor. Tears started. And once they started, she couldn't seem to stop them. She curled up on the hardwood and sobbed into her fist until her head pounded and her lungs ached. Drained, she got to her feet.

The sofa beckoned, but as soon as she landed there

everything she'd run from piled on. She shot up and walked to the window. Then back to the sofa, then to the window again.

Pacing her living room left her fidgety and exhausted, but every time she stopped moving the appalling scene from the rehearsal dinner replayed in her mind—Mommy Dearest stumbling in, spewing venom while everyone within earshot stared on in horror or fascination. Worse, the look on Booker's face haunted her. She didn't need to imagine what he thought of her right now. His shuttered expression told her better than words.

Her fault. She could blame Denise for being a malicious drunk, and ruining his family's happy occasion without the slightest hesitation, but she couldn't blame her mother for the rest. Underneath all the woman's insults and rage lay the ugly truth.

She'd fucked up completely—even in her one noble intention of keeping Booker at a safe distance from her mistakes. Her worst-case scenarios never included watching the ticking time bomb she'd failed to defuse explode all over him. She'd known the fallout was going to hurt like hell, but she hadn't counted on him being right there at ground zero with her while his poor family looked on.

The knowledge cut deep—past her pain, and her battered conscience, and straight to her soul. She had to fix this. Apologize. She didn't know how, but prowling around her apartment wasn't going to get it done. Screw it. She'd drive over to the sheriff's department and wait. The worst he could do was send her away.

Propelled by purpose, she grabbed her purse from the floor, pulled her front door open, and…stopped short. Her heart bounced around in her chest and then sank heavily to her stomach. Booker stood there, jaw tight, eyes dark, fist lifted in mid-knock.

• • •

Red-rimmed eyes moved over him, wary and urgent at the same time. She stepped back and wrapped her arms around her middle, turning herself into a beautiful, devastated island. "Booker. Come in."

He shut the door behind him and then turned to her. A part of him wanted to shake her senseless, and then do whatever it took to erase the misery from her face. But touching her now, defaulting to the one connection they had that she could never deny, avoided the real issues.

"I'm sorry," she whispered.

The soft words, the obvious truth in them, banked his temper—somewhat. "What, specifically, are you apologizing for, Jailbait?"

She let out a miserable laugh and flung her arm in an all-encompassing gesture. "Everything…my mother showing up drunk and ruining your sister's rehearsal dinner."

Yeah, that wasn't what he wanted to hear. Fixating on the ruined rehearsal dinner was like fixating on the tip of an iceberg. Despite the last ten years and six weeks spent proving she could rely on him, her natural instinct when faced with a problem was still to put her guard up and block anyone who might try to help. Including him. Whether it stemmed from pride or fear didn't much matter. It came down to a lack of trust, and if he didn't call her on it, nothing would change. "You have no control over or responsibility for your mother's behavior. Try again."

She looked down, and worried her cuticle. "I'm sorry for not telling you she contacted me, and why."

Okay, now they were getting somewhere. "Why didn't you? We agreed your mother was a problem I could help solve. You promised to pull me in the next time she contacted you."

Still looking down, she shrugged. "I guess you'd call it taking the fifth."

"I don't think that's the reason, but we can detour there since you bring it up." He pulled a folded document from his jacket and handed it to her.

"What's this?" Shaking fingers closed on the paper.

"The good news I had for you. The insurance company sent Nelson a copy of their report."

She skimmed it while he waited, slowly settling on the arm of the sofa as the information sank in. Then her eyes found his. "Their investigator agreed it was an electrical short?"

He nodded. "In the circuit behind your refrigerator. Old wires serving too much voltage. The fire started behind the wall and burned up and out. It's irrelevant whether you were in the bakery that morning, because nobody can move a thousand pound fridge, fuck with the outlet in an undetectable way, and then move it back to exactly the same footprint without leaving a single scratch or nick on the floor."

She let out a long, shuddering breath. The report fluttered like a leaf in her hand. "I honestly didn't have anything to do with the fire."

"I know. I never thought you did. I never would have thought otherwise, even if I'd had all the facts. Why didn't you tell me the whole truth that morning? Who were you trying to protect?"

Stormy eyes flickered his way. "Me…and *you*."

"I'm not the vulnerable one in this scenario." He said the words firmly. "I've got a badge, and all the power and authority behind it. As of now your mother's under arrest for DUI, public intoxication, trespassing, and battery. She also has an outstanding bench warrant with Los Angeles Superior Court for failing to appear in another matter, and the neighbor she 'borrowed' the car from reported it as stolen." He closed in on her. "She's out of action for a while. Longer if you tack on a blackmail charge."

"It doesn't matter." Defeat dragged at her voice. "Eventually she'll shoot out the other end of this, and she'll be back. As long as she's alive and kicking, I'm always going to have a target on my ass."

The resignation in her voice rekindled his temper. "Bullshit." The word came out. "When she shows up, I'll bust her again. And again, if necessary. I can play that game for as long as it takes to show her there's no winning. When I told you to let me know the next time she contacted you, that wasn't my ego talking. I'm in a position to make it impossible for her to get to you, just by doing my job. If you'd been honest with me weeks ago, everything tonight could have been avoided."

She prowled the room like a caged animal. "I was ashamed, all right? My mother mortifies me. The only reason Denise creeps into my life is to bleed me for money. Nothing I have is off-limits. Not my reputation. Not my business. Not my... friends. That's the kind of person I come from. I'm ashamed of her. Worse, I'm ashamed of the level she pulls me down to every time she comes around. She threatens something I care about, and I pay. I *hate* the kind of person it makes me. I hate feeling weak and desperate and under her fucking thumb. I've spent my life keeping the whole pathetic situation out of people's view, because..." She broke off, sagged against the wall, and rubbed the heel of her hand over her forehead. "You wouldn't understand."

His heart hurt for her, standing there with her back in a corner, looking alone and miserable. The thing to remember was she'd backed herself into that corner, and she'd have to take the steps to get herself out. Even so, he closed the distance. "You might be surprised what I understand, if you mustered up the courage to tell me."

"How in God's name would you understand?" Her head snapped up. "You come from a different world, Booker. The reality is you've never"—she swept her hand through the air, clearing an invisible surface—"*never* had to compromise your morals, ethics, or anything else to protect something you care about. That's not a trust issue. It's a simple reality."

And there it was. The rest of the iceberg, and not a damn thing he could do to change the shape of it, because it was *him*. "No." Suddenly he was bone tired. Tired of the ache in his chest and the burn in his gut. "I've had advantages. I can't deny that—hell, I'm thankful for them—but I know what it means to work for something I wanted. Nobody handed me a badge. I earned it. Still, some people can't see past the advantages. I know that, and for the most part I don't give a shit, but I never thought you'd be one of them."

"Booker—"

"Since you're such a fan of reality, let me give you some more. I love you."

She flinched. "Don't—"

He braced his hands on the wall on either side of her head and kept talking. "Whether you want to admit it or not, you love me, too. But you don't want to. You don't want to be vulnerable. You don't want to trust. At heart, you're the same scared, defensive kid I pulled off the beach ten years ago."

Her hand landed on his chest, over his heart, as if to protect it. She blinked, and a tear trickled down her cheek. "I'm sorry."

Dammit to hell. He rested his forehead against hers for a moment, and breathed her in. Then he forced himself to straighten. "I don't want you to be sorry, Lauralie. I want you to grow up."

Unfortunately, only one of them could make that happen, and it wasn't him. He only had one move left, so he made it.

He walked away.

Chapter Sixteen

Thirty minutes spent getting Maytagged in rough, five-foot surf synchronized mind and body—just not the way Laurie had hoped. She'd grabbed her board and taken refuge in the ocean at dawn, looking for an escape from the endless churn of her thoughts. Instead of emerging energized and clearheaded, she trudged up the shore utterly wrung out.

After laying her board on the sand, she sat, tugged open the neck closure on her wetsuit, and wrangled the zipper down a few inches. The efforts did little to relieve the strangled sensation plaguing her since the moment yesterday evening when Denise had stumbled into the restaurant. She rested her arms on her bent knees and squinted at the water while memories tumbled through her mind like breaking waves.

Booker accused her of being the same girl he'd dragged off this beach ten years ago, emotionally at least, but it was true in a lot of other ways, too. All the time she'd spent scraping and scrambling to make something of herself hadn't gotten her very far. She was grown up enough to know that much.

A seagull screeched overhead, startling her. She released a breath and dug in her bag for her phone. Maybe Chelsea had texted with a meet time for later today. Thanking her for offering up her bonus, and then explaining why it wouldn't help, after all, wouldn't be easy, but just seeing her best friend would level her out. Chelsea had that effect on people.

The screen lit with a new message. Her fingers trembled as she read the communication from the insurance adjuster. He thanked her for her updated statement, and advised her they'd completed their investigation. The evidence concerning the cause of the fire conclusively pointed to a short in the wiring. A check for the total amount of her claim was in process. Some legal mumbo jumbo followed, but she barely skimmed it because, holy crap, she'd actually managed to rescue something she'd almost blown.

"Mind if I join you?"

Laurie jolted, and turned to find Rebecca Booker standing there. She shook her head, but inwardly braced for a confrontation. She had it coming after last night.

Booker's mother executed a graceful descent and took a seat beside her, absently brushing sand off the knee of her workout leggings. "I came down for a run on the beach this morning and spotted the Babycakes logo on the SUV in the parking area. I figured you were nearby."

Who knew the Expedition was such a mom magnet? She doubted an apology would cut short whatever dressing down was coming her way, but she owed the woman a big one, and now was probably her best chance to offer it. "I'm sorry about last night."

Rebecca frowned. "So you said last night, and then rushed off before I could reply. I'll tell you now what I would have told you then, if you'd stuck around. I don't want your apology."

"Fair enough, but it's all I've got. I can't turn back time

and un-ruin the dinner—"

"You misunderstand." Dark hair gleamed in the sun as she shook her head. "You didn't ruin anything. First of all, it takes more than an over-served party crasher to get between my family and a good meal. Second, even if the disruption had ruined the dinner, it wouldn't be you who owed an apology. It would be your mother. Now, if she wants to send me an apology, I'll happily accept it, but yours?" She waved her hand. "Unwarranted."

The tightness in her chest loosened a fraction. "That's nice of you to say."

She waved her hand again, batting the comment away. "It's the truth. Will we see you at the wedding this evening?"

"Um…no." She forced a laugh and sank her fingers into the sand. "I'm sure that comes as a relief. I know I don't fit your brand."

Rebecca shrugged. "You fit Booker's brand, and that's what's important."

The tightness in her chest came back with a vengeance. "I don't. I'm not the kind of woman he needs."

"When it comes to my son, I only know one thing. He's quite capable of deciding for himself what he needs." She sifted sand through her manicured fingers. "Don't expect me to repeat that too often, because admitting as much goes against my natural instincts. I specialize in telling people how to live happy, healthy, fulfilling lives, and as a result, I tend to think I know what's best for everyone. Most of the time I do, so I'm not likely to change my ways, but Booker is an exception."

"He's wrong this time. He deserves more than—"

"The woman he loves?" Rebecca challenged.

"I—It's not that simple."

His mother got to her feet, and brushed the sand off the seat of her pants. "No. Like most important things in life, love takes strength and courage. I wouldn't have pegged you as lacking either. I hope you don't prove me wrong."

. . .

"You know, Booker, a lot of people find weddings happy occasions. Some even crack a smile."

He turned to see Aaron step onto the patio of the pool house the groom and his entourage had been relegated to until the appointed hour.

"I'm happy," he said, and resumed his study of the bougainvillea leaves floating on the calm blue water of the pool.

Aaron came up beside him and rested his hands on the iron railing separating the patio from the pool. "Yeah, that's why you look like you want to bust somebody. I don't want that surly expression standing up with me on what's supposed to be the happiest fucking day of my life. It makes me nervous. Come on." He punched Booker in the shoulder. "Talk it out, mate."

Booker grunted from the slug. "There's nothing to talk out."

"Sure there is. Tell you what, I'll start. Delightful meeting Laurie's mum last night."

"That's one word for it." Resigned to the discussion, he turned to face Aaron and folded his arms across his chest.

"Have the situation contained, do we?"

"Yep." Just thinking about it pissed him off. He pushed away from the rail and crossed the patio, trying to walk off the frustration. "I could have contained it weeks ago if she'd told me what was going on, but no. Why confide in me? I'm only the sheriff."

Aaron turned and leaned back against the railing. "She's embarrassed."

"I don't give a shit." He pivoted and strode toward rail again. "I *love* her, goddammit. I expect her to come to me when she needs help, not hide things from me like I'm an enemy. I'm on her side, and if I haven't proved that much to her by now, then, damn it"—he banged a support post with the side of his fist, hard enough to feel the impact all the way up his arm—"I'm fucked."

"She thinks of you as the enemy? Those were her words?"

"Her actions told me. All she said was that I wouldn't understand."

Aaron blew out a breath and took a step back. "I want to point out something, but before I do, keep this in mind. Kate will rip my balls off if either of us shows up to this wedding with a black eye."

"Noted."

"Good. What I want to point out is, she's not entirely wrong."

"I haven't proved I'm on her side?" He dragged a hand through his hair to keep from smacking the post again. "That's bullshit—"

"No, not the 'on her side' part." He shook his head. "She's not entirely wrong saying you don't understand. Women are complex mysteries, mate. Like black holes or the plot of *Fight Club*. They defy understanding. Blokes are basic."

Frustration propelled him across the patio again. "I've known her for a long time. I spent a lot of years trying to be in her corner, and protect her—from herself, half the time. I flat-out reject the notion I don't understand her. I understand her better than she understands herself."

"Uh-uh. You see her more objectively than she sees herself, but that's entirely different."

"You barely know her." Bracing his shoulders against the stucco wall, he challenged his future brother-in-law. "And just so we're clear, the accent doesn't make you some kind of an authority on women." Everything about this conversation set his teeth on edge. Especially the insinuation there was some gap between Lauralie and him that could never be bridged, no matter what he did. *But haven't you reached the same conclusion? Isn't that why you left last night?*

Aaron sank his hands into his pockets and looked down at the toes of his polished black shoes. After a moment of internal debate, his eyes landed on Booker. "My dear pop was a raging alcoholic, as well as a right bastard."

Well shit. Now he felt like a prick, making his friend dredge up a painful past on his wedding day. "Okay. I get it. You have a perspective on shitty upbringings that I'll never have. We don't have to go there."

The corner of Aaron's mouth quirked up. "Grab a seat, Booker." He nodded toward the round, wrought iron patio table surrounded by four matching chairs. "We're going there. You're family—will be in a few hours as I've survived all the hazing—so now you sit while I do my filial duty and pull your head out of your arse."

"All right. Fine." He dragged the closest chair out, wincing as metal scraped brick, and dropped into the seat. "Welcome to the family."

"Cheers. Do you know if anyone had told me a year ago I'd be wedding Kate Booker on Saint Valentine's Day with God as my witness, I would have laughed 'til I pissed myself?"

"I'm sure she'd be flattered to hear that."

"Don't take me wrong. I *wanted* her the moment I saw her. I aimed to get a leg over—"

"Keep talking, and you're going to end up with a black eye after all—"

"I was a bit of a lad," Aaron went on, "and I liked it that way."

Booker propped his forearms on his knees. This was starting to sound familiar. "But you changed. You met the right woman, and you changed."

"I fell for her against my will, and it scared the shite out of me. Kate's posh and polished, and I'm some git from Hackney. I pushed her back more than once because I couldn't make sense of us. I knew happy relationships existed, in theory, but where I come from, they're like unicorns—rare and magical—and I reckoned I didn't have a hell of a lot of magic in me. Yeah, I was testing her, but mostly doubting me. I didn't trust myself with something good."

Lauralie's words echoed in his ears. *It's not you I don't trust. It's me.* "How did you get past the self-doubt?"

Aaron laughed. "Have you met the women in your brood? Kate's got a lot of her mum in her. Once she sets her sights on something, game over. She didn't give me ultimatums, but she saw right through my gobshite. Nothing short of me saying, 'I don't love you,' was going to shake her. I couldn't say those words, because I did love her, and she knew it."

Booker rubbed the center of his chest, and the empty ache lodged there since yesterday evening. "She didn't let you fuck things up."

"Brilliant way of putting it."

Chapter Seventeen

Laurie stepped out of her SUV, took a ticket from the red-vested valet, and smoothed a hand down the fitted skirt of her red dress. A Valentine's Day wedding kind of demanded the color.

A path of rose petals in varying shades of red led guests to the entrance of the main house. The large, carved doors hung open, welcoming arrivals, and greeters hovered to lead guests through the house to the grounds beyond where the ceremony would take place. She paused by the door, waiting in the small line of guests backed up there, feeling a little like a roller coaster rider white-knuckling the restraining bar while the cart inched up to the first big drop.

Then again, she ought to be numb to the dread, considering the last twenty-four hours had been a nonstop roller coaster. At least this time she purposefully boarded the ride.

Part of the reason had to do with Rebecca's words that morning. Booker knew what he wanted. The only thing she ought to be asking herself was whether she had the strength and courage to go after what *she* wanted.

Another part of the decision stemmed from meeting with Chelsea earlier in the afternoon. Seeing her friend, absorbing the love and support she offered simply by existing, and giving the same back, had gone a long way toward reminding her some relationships in her life actually worked. Chelsea believed in her, firmly enough to invest fifty thousand dollars of her hard-earned money in Babycakes. It had felt good—stabilizing—to stand together with her best friend in the empty Ocean Avenue unit they both liked for the new home of their business, and focus on the future. Even better when Chelsea had admitted the future involved her moving back to Montenido.

She'd worried she'd spoil the triumphant moment by crying all over her friend about Booker, but it had turned out to be Chelsea who'd needed the shoulder to cry on.

Laurie had fully supported Chelsea's decision to start fresh in Maui after enduring the most fucked-up breakup in history with another undeserving asshole. She'd sent her friend off with the advice to guard her battered heart, banish her inner good girl, and concentrate on enjoying loads of five-star sex with Rafe St. Sebastian. She'd done exactly as Laurie instructed, except somewhere between the multiple orgasms, she'd fallen in love with the man, but was too scared of admitting it to herself—much less Rafe—and opening herself to the risk of rejection.

Instead of glowing with accomplishment, Chelsea had stood there blinking back tears.

The conversation replayed in her mind as she followed one of the greeters through the house. Chelsea had declared her fresh start a failure, because she hadn't guarded her heart. Laurie had been compelled to tell her the whole guarded-heart thing didn't really work. It was just a chickenshit way of trying not to get hurt.

Ultimately she'd convinced Chelsea to dig up some

courage and tell Rafe how she felt. As she'd uttered the word, she'd realized courage — or lack thereof — had become a major theme in her life. Too many of her decisions had been motivated by fear and shame.

Some residual shame burned inside her now as she followed the greeter through the house. Booker deserved an explanation. Most importantly, he was entitled to three words, freely spoken. She loved him. After that, she honestly didn't know what to expect. She had fucked things up — possibly beyond repair — but if he'd give her a second chance, she'd do whatever it took to show him her love was stronger than her fear.

The greeter led her to the back patio, and handed her off to a tuxedo-clad usher. He, in turn, steered her along the rose petal path that led down the center of an expansive, linen-draped tent encompassing two large banks of white chairs already crowded with guests, and directed her to an empty seat in a middle row.

At the end of the aisle, beyond a white pergola, the first peachy tinges of sunset decorated the blue horizon. The scent of roses sweetened the ocean breeze fluttering through the open-sided tent. The light wind caused an occasional shower of petals from the festoons of blossoms woven through the thousands of tiny lights strung overhead. A scattering of the velvety confetti drifted down, decorating the older couple occupying the chairs to her left, and the threesome of women in their early twenties who claimed the seats on her right. Their giggling conversation blended with the strains of a string quartet playing under an arbor positioned just beyond the groom-side seating, but she picked up enough to glean they worked for Rebecca.

The prelude changed to Pachelbel's Canon, and the officiant made his way down the aisle. The hum of conversation subsided. Next came Booker's mom, looking stunning in a sheer-sleeved claret gown. Then the groom strode down the aisle, followed by the groomsmen. Restless nerves migrated from her stomach to her chest as her eyes landed on Booker. He focused ahead, and didn't see her, which left her free to drink in the sight of him looking handsome, and remote, and completely out of her league.

The blonde three seats over sighed. "Groomsmen on parade…best part of every wedding, and look, not a ring in the bunch. They're all bachelors."

"I'll take bachelor number three," the other blonde whispered, and Laurie realized she meant Booker.

"Choose again," the redhead said. "That's Ethan Booker, and Rebecca told me he's off the market."

"Really? Since when?"

Red shrugged. "Earlier today. Said she could cross finding the perfect woman for Booker off her to-do list, because he'd done the job himself—the woman just didn't quite know it yet."

"Damn. I'd be willing to let him convince me. He wouldn't even have to work very hard."

Laurie bit her tongue to keep from breaking into the conversation and telling the blonde to back off. No, she wasn't perfect—far from it—but if he gave her the chance, she'd show him she *was* the perfect woman for him.

The other blonde laughed. "That's part of your charm, Bridget. You're easy."

"Hey, now—"

"Shh!"

The quartet transitioned into Mendelssohn and everyone stood and turned to watch the bride and her father walk down the aisle through a lazy rain of rose petals.

Kate looked beautiful in a slim, white column of silk. Beside her, Richard beamed. A subdued chorus of sighs and some sniffles sounded as they passed.

When they reached the altar, the guests sat. Richard kissed his daughter, hugged Aaron, and took his seat in the first row next to Rebecca. The officiant welcomed everyone. Laurie did her best to focus on the ceremony, but her gaze kept drifting to the right like a swimmer caught in a riptide. The words of the ceremony faded as she concentrated on fighting the pull. After a few moments she gave in to the inevitable and let her attention slide to Booker, only to get a hard little jolt when she found his dark eyes staring back at her.

Her heart stumbled, and then raced. She searched his face for some clue of his emotions, but his expression gave nothing away. Nor did it waver.

From what seemed like a thousand miles away, the officiant intoned, "We've reached the 'speak now or forever hold your peace' point in the ceremony, but I'm not a stickler for tradition, and, well….Kate and Aaron aren't particularly interested in hearing any reasons they shouldn't be married."

He paused while the guests chuckled, then added, "Instead, they'd like to invite you to share your words of wisdom and love with them."

A few hands went up. The officiant nodded at a silver-haired man near the front. A young woman in a red dress brought a microphone over. The man stood and said, "I'll start by laying out my credentials. Elise"—he gestured at the sweet little old woman beside him—"and I will celebrate forty-three years of wedded bliss next month." He paused to accept applause before continuing. "So, you know, we might have learned a lesson or two about how to make a relationship last. I think it comes down to three things. Listen to each other, always find a compromise, and—"

"Lots of sex!" Elise interjected.

Everyone laughed and clapped. When the officiant recovered, he motioned to a woman a few rows ahead on the groom's side. She stood, holding a blanket-wrapped newborn, and waited until Miss Microphone tilted the mic at her before greeting the room.

"Hey, Kate. Hey, Aaron. Congratulations. We're all so happy for you." The comment brought a quick round of endorsing applause. "I wanted to tell you never to give up on each other, or the dreams you share. Even when the odds seem stacked against you." She lifted the baby a little higher in her arms, and smiled. "Love can make dreams come true."

While onlookers applauded, she sat. The sandy-haired man beside the new mom wrapped his arm around her shoulder, kissed her, and then the baby.

Laurie snuck a glance at Booker. He caught her looking. After a suspended second one brow cocked up in a silent challenge. The officiant asked if anyone else would like to speak. Laurie raised her hand before her mind realized her body had gone rogue.

Wait. This isn't your best idea...

He pointed to her and nodded.

Okay. Fuck it. Let's do this.

She stood on wobbling legs and cleared her throat while every eye in the crowd turned to her. In the second row of the bride's side, Miranda McQueen scowled and muttered something to the equally dour woman sitting beside her.

Simmer down, bitches. I'm here until Booker tells me to go.

The attendant handed her the microphone. She wrapped her sweaty palm around the grip and did her best to hold it steady. "Hi. I'm Laurie and, um, I don't have forty-three years of marriage as a credential, or a baby, but I recently learned an important lesson about love. It...uh..." God, why was it so hot in February? She wiped her forehead and cleared her throat. "It takes courage. Courage you obviously have, since you're standing up there ready to pledge yourselves to each other."

The observation brought a smattering of applause. She

used the moment to catch her breath, but then her eyes reconnected with Booker's and the intensity of his gaze left her winded again. "Not everyone has the courage. I didn't. I guarded my heart. Pretty much from everyone, but especially from a certain man who always seemed to be there when I needed someone. He always had my back. I took his help—not graciously, I'm ashamed to admit, but I took it—and I relied on his strength, but when it came to love, I pushed him away. I told him he didn't understand me. I told him he *couldn't* understand me. But it was a lie. He understands me better than anyone."

Silence met her confession. The trickle of a fountain in the distance became unnaturally loud. She swallowed, and gave voice to the question silently thrown at her from every direction. "What kind of self-sabotaging idiot does that?"

The salty sting of tears blurred her vision, but not before she saw Booker step out of line and make his way down the aisle toward her. Heads turned to watch him close the distance.

She licked her lips, and started talking faster. "One who lets fear rule her life. I thought, deep down, I really didn't have as much to offer him as he offered me, and certainly not everything he deserved, but I was wrong, because… because…" She trailed off as Booker drew even with her row.

He extended a hand to her. "I've waited a long time to hear this, Jailbait. Get over here and say it to my face."

Her feet refused to move. The blonde beside her stood, gave her a small shove, and stage-whispered, "I swear to God, if you don't get your butt over there and tell the man you love him, I'm going to hurdle you and say it myself."

That put her into motion, even as a tension-relieving laugh rippled through the onlookers. She squeezed past the older couple, stumbling a little as she reached for Booker. And then he had her in his arms, holding her tight enough she could count the rock-steady beats of his heart. She looked up at him, blinked the tears away, and pulled his face into focus. "I love you, Booker. It's always been you. From the first time you stood up for my scared, reckless, and secretly grateful ass, I knew you were the one. If you give me another chance, I'll spend every day of the rest of my life proving it to y—"

His kiss cut her off—the warm, certain press of his lips like a vow against hers. The last of her anxiety disintegrated into a thunder of relief and need. It wasn't until he raised his head and smiled down at her that she realized the thunder wasn't just in her head. All around them, guests applauded. He gave her another kiss—short but just as potent—and then his mouth found her ear. "I love you, Lauralie, and I'll give you as many chances as it takes. Promise you'll do the same for me. Neither one of us will let the other fuck this up, okay?"

She drew back and nodded. "I promise."

"Good." He tipped his head toward the altar. "I better get back up there."

"Duty calls."

"Yeah. Don't go anywhere."

"I'm not going anywhere. I want forty-three years. I want shared dreams, I want—"

"Lots of sex?" The corner of his mouth and one eyebrow shot up in a look guaranteed to get him all the sex he could handle.

"I hear it's the secret to a lasting relationship."

He hauled her into his arms for another long, slow kiss. A few catcalls and whistles sounded when he finally raised his head. His voice vibrated in her ear.

"Jailbait, this relationship is going last forever."

Epilogue

"Oh, yeah, I want it. All of it. Don't make me beg."

Laurie looked up from replenishing a tower of mini-bundts to find Arden St. Sebastian staring longingly at the display case. Behind her, a small crowd of people packed into Babycakes by the Beach, celebrating this evening's preview before tomorrow's grand opening.

Before Laurie could respond, Chelsea appeared and swept Arden into a hug. The big, shiny diamond decorating her best friend's finger glinted in the overhead light, and Laurie couldn't help but smile. Chelsea's attempt at a no-strings fling with Rafe St. Sebastian had failed spectacularly, and she'd never been happier. "Hey! I'm so glad you could make it. Have you met Laurie?"

"Pleasure," Laurie said, extending a hand to Chelsea's future sister-in-law, and trying not to feel guilty about wanting to bitch-slap the dark-haired beauty the night of the Las Ventanas party.

"The pleasure is all mine. Seriously." Arden eyed the case again. "I found my happy place the minute I walked through the door. I want to move in. I'll bunk right here." She tapped the glass, indicating the upper shelf of the display case holding a selection of small, frosted cakes.

"Wait." Laurie handed her a chocolate-glazed chocolate bundt. "You should try before you pack your bags."

Arden took a big bite, and then closed her eyes and groaned. "Oh. My. God. That is the closest I've come to an orgasm in…I can't even remember. I'll take a dozen. No, wait. Two dozen."

She laughed, and nodded to one of the employees she'd been able to rehire, who began filling a box with cakes. "You need to get out more. Good as these are, nothing beats a real orgasm."

"Truth," Chelsea nodded.

"Girl, if I'm ever going to have a shot at it, you've got to stop my brother from buying hotels. Between work, and"— she paused, and then waved her hand as if swatting the thought away— "more work, I haven't had a moment to play, much less find a playmate."

"Aren't you headed to Maui soon?" Chelsea asked. "I guarantee you a week at St. Sebastian's newest resort will solve that little problem."

Arden shook her head, and gave Laurie a wry smile. "My life looks fabulous on paper. I'm flying out this week, but it's more work. Help put the St. Sebastian stamp on the property and keep my father from forgetting he stepped down as chairman of the board."

Chelsea grinned. "Good luck with that—"

"Congratulations, ladies!"

Laurie turned to see Kate and Aaron cutting through the crowd. They walked hand in hand, glowing their newlywed glow, despite returning from their honeymoon almost two months ago. The glow might well be permanent, she theorized, as she automatically searched beyond them for Booker. She pushed past a little eddy of disappointment when she didn't spy him. "Hey, you two. Great to see you."

"We wouldn't miss your big night," Kate assured her, and then leaned over to hug Chelsea and Arden.

"Damn right," Aaron agreed. "The missus promised me cake and a shag."

Kate thumped him in the chest with the back of her hand, but Laurie just laughed.

"Well, I can help with the cake part."

"Jesus. Everybody's getting laid except me," Arden complained.

"Still involuntarily celibate?" Kate's eyes went wide. "Don't mention that to my mother, unless you want a bag of DIY."

"Not necessary," Arden replied, and lifted the last bite of her cake. "I found a perfectly satisfying substitute."

"Cheers, love, but I feel obliged to point out, some of us manage to 'ave both."

While Arden chewed on that, Laurie asked the question she'd been trying to stifle since Kate and Aaron walked in. "Um…where's Booker?"

They glanced at each other—quick, but she caught the look—before Kate said, "He's running late. He told us to tell you he'll be over as soon as he can get away."

Disappointment swirled again, but she refused to let it suck her in. Being sheriff wasn't a clock-in, clock-out kind of job. Sometimes he got held up, and—

"Lauralie, I *love* this place!" A woman's voice cut through the din, and the next thing she knew, she was wrapped in a cloud of Pima cotton and custom-blended organic perfume. After a moment, Rebecca drew back and smiled at her. "Congratulations, honey."

"Thank you." She expanded her smile to include Richard, and added, "Thanks for coming."

"Of course we came."

"I wasn't sure…you know, with the brand and all, but, I have a surprise for you."

"A surprise, for us?"

"Yep. Hold on. Don't go anywhere." She hurried to the other display case, grabbed two pink pastry boxes, and handed them to Booker's parents.

Rebecca's eyebrows shot up. "What's this?" she asked as she opened the box and stared at the decadent chocolate treat.

"They're grain-free, refined-sugar-free chocolate peppermint bars. I used the Best Life organic cocoa, and—"

"And they're wonderful," Rebecca finished the sentence around a mouthful of chocolate. "I can't believe you did this."

"I wanted to offer something for everyone. You should be able to treat yourself with a clean conscience. Right now I've only got a handful of items, but I'm hoping to expand if demand is good."

"Demand will be great, if this is anything to go by," Richard said after swallowing his sample, and then hugged his wife. "Darling, this is the best idea you never had."

"Shhh. Don't tell anyone I didn't think of it. I have a reputation to uphold."

The rest of their conversation faded as the energy in the bakery changed. She couldn't explain how exactly, but the air quickened, the molecules became supercharged. She turned and looked toward the front of the shop.

Booker stood just inside the door, wearing his uniform—a sight always guaranteed to kick her pulse up a notch—and a hint of a smile. While she watched, he tipped his head toward the sidewalk. A silent message. *Come with me.*

Before she could formulate a response, Chelsea put a hand on her shoulder and said, "Go on. Take a break. The team and I can handle things here."

. . .

Booker watched Lauralie peel off her Babycakes apron and hand it to one of the girls behind the counter before making her way to the door. She stopped to accept some hugs and congratulations along the way, but finally came to a stop in front of him. A smile lifted the corner of her mouth. "Is there a problem, Sheriff?"

Behind her, Aaron, Kate, Chelsea, and his parents sent him thumbs up. He refrained from rolling his eyes. Aaron couldn't keep a fucking secret. "I'm afraid I'm going to have to ask you to step outside."

Her eyebrow lifted, but she shrugged and walked through the door he held open for her. When it clicked shut behind them, he turned and simply drank in the sight of her for a second. She couldn't know how breathtaking she looked standing in the semicircle of light cast from the bakery, radiating with pride and happiness. He hated to dim it for even a second, but hoped by the time he finished saying the things that needed to be said, the radiant flush would be back—stronger than ever. "Congratulations, Jailbait. It looks like you've got a success on your hands."

Her smile softened. "I couldn't have done it without you."

"Not true." He shook his head and took her hand. "It might have taken you a little longer, but you would have done it. Sorry I'm late."

"No problem. Kate told me you got held up. Nothing serious, I hope."

"Just information. I got a call from one of my friends in the DA's office in LA" He wove his fingers between hers. "Your mother plead guilty to trespassing, auto theft, and DUI in exchange for sixteen months in county."

Her hand stiffened. "I'll mark my calendar."

"There's no need. In or out, she can't hurt you. The people

who care about you won't let it happen. *I* won't let it happen. You're beyond her reach. I simply wanted you to know."

"All right." The words came out on a measured exhale. Then she surprised him by going up onto her tiptoes. "Thanks for telling me." Her lips brushed the corner of his mouth. "Thanks for having my back." She kissed the other corner. "And thanks for reminding me I'm not alone." She planted a kiss squarely on his lips. A long, slow, surrender of a kiss he felt himself sliding into. Before the invitation became too much to resist, he reluctantly eased away.

"I thought you could use a better reminder."

"A better…what?" Her eyelids fluttered open and her brows knit with confusion.

"A better reminder you're not alone." He took a step back, reached into his pocket, and cast an irritated glance at the faces pressed to the bakery window, watching them. "Even when you want to be."

Her breath hitched as he pulled out the ring. The blue diamond he'd chosen because it reminded him of her eyes gleamed in the low light.

"Oh, my God, Booker. Do you know what you're getting yourself into?"

"Lauralie, I know exactly what I'm doing. After ten years, I know *you* inside and out. I know you dream big, and you work relentlessly to make those dreams a reality. I know you've got a hard head, and a smart mouth. I also know you've got a big, soft, reckless heart. And I need all of it. I love you, and I want to spend the rest of my life with you—"

That's as far as he got before she launched herself into his arms, and he had to stagger back a step to keep them on their feet. From the other side of the glass, hoots and applause erupted.

"Yes," she whispered between raining kisses in the general vicinity of his mouth. "I love you, too. I think I started to fall for you ten years ago when you marched me off that beach down there and called me on my bullshit. I needed that. I needed you. I've grown up since then, and I've changed a lot, but that part will never change. I need you. I spent a long time fighting the need because I thought it made me weak, but it doesn't. It makes me strong. *You* make me strong."

People began spilling out onto the sidewalk, his mother in the lead. "Strong enough to handle my family, Jailbait?"

"Strong enough to handle anything," she promised, and kissed him with abandon as he slid their symbol of forever onto her finger.

Acknowledgments

This book was a struggle to write. I'm not talking figuratively, I mean literally. I had a little pain in my neck that turned into a big pain in everyone's ass, and I missed all my deadlines. Instead of telling me what a big, unreliable loser I was, the lovely people at Entangled offered me time and encouragement. Thank you to Liz, Curtis, and especially Heather. I can't tell you how much I appreciate your patience.

Big additional thanks to:

The rest of the Entangled team. Even if you hear it every day, it needs to be repeated. You are the best!

The Romance Writers of America and the Los Angeles Romance Authors. They taught me everything I know about romance.

The readers. You've made me a better writer. I try to bring it for you, every…single…time.

To my family. You've made me a better woman.

To Robin and Hayson. I'm not even going to try to be funny this time. I love you guys. (Insert mic drop here).

About the Author

Wine lover, sleep fanatic, and *USA Today* Bestselling Author of sexy contemporary romance novels, Samanthe Beck lives in Malibu, California, with her long-suffering but extremely adorable husband and their turbo-son. Throw in a furry ninja named Kitty and Bebe the trash talking Chihuahua and you get the whole, chaotic picture.

When not dreaming up fun, fan-your-cheeks sexy ways to get her characters to happily-ever-after, she searches for the perfect cabernet to pair with Ambien.

A Fool for You

a *Foolproof Love* novel by Katee Robert

It's been thirteen years since Hope Moore left Devil's Falls, land of sexy cowboys and bad memories. Back for the weekend, she has no intention of seeing Daniel Rodriguez, the man she never got over, or for the two of them getting down and dirty. It's just a belated goodbye, right? No harm, no foul. Until six weeks later, when her pregnancy test comes back positive...

His Best Mistake

a *Shillings Agency* novel by Diane Alberts

One night with a stranger... Security expert Mark Matthews has loved, and lost, and has no intention of ever loving again — especially not a woman who thrives on her life being in danger. Now, hot, meaningless sex with strangers he had no intention of ever seeing again? That's a whole other story. And it's all life as a single father allows him to enjoy. But when he meets Daisy O'Rourke, the game is on, because she's everything he swore to stay away from. She has bad idea written all over her, but he's in too deep to walk away now...

Playing it Cool

a *Sydney Smoke Rugby* novel by Amy Andrews

Harper Nugent might have a little extra junk in her trunk, but her stepbrother calling her out on it is the last straw... When rugby hottie, Dexter Blake, witnesses the insult, he surprises Harper by asking her out. In front of her dumbass brother. Score! Of course, she knows it's not for reals, but Dex won't take no for an answer. Still the date is better than either expected. So is the next one. And the next. And the heat between them...sizzles their clothes right off. Suddenly, this fake relationship is feeling all too real...

Discover the **Compromise Me** *series…*

COMPROMISING HER POSITION

Also by Samanthe Beck

PRIVATE PRACTICE

LIGHT HER FIRE

FALLING FOR THE ENEMY

LOVER UNDERCOVER

FALLING FOR THE MARINE

WICKED GAMES

BEST MAN WITH BENEFITS

CPSIA information can be obtained
at www.ICGtesting.com
Printed in the USA
LVOW10s1625201216
518113LV00001B/25/P